The
CODE BUSTERS
CLUB

CASE #1:

The Secret of the
Skeleton Key

The
CODE BUSTERS
CLUB

CASE #1:

The Secret of the Skeleton Key

Penny Warner

EGMONT
USA
New York

EGMONT

We bring stories to life

First published by Egmont USA, 2011
443 Park Avenue South, Suite 806
New York, NY 10016

1 3 5 7 9 8 6 4 2

www.egmontusa.com
www.pennywarner.com
www.CodeBustersClub.com

Library of Congress Cataloging-in-Publication Data
Warner, Penny.
    The secret of the skeleton key / Penny Warner.
        p. cm. — (The Code Busters Club ; Case #1)
    Summary: Using their code-breaking skills, four middle-schoolers
solve the mystery of the eccentric man who draws stick figures on his
second-floor bedroom window.
    ISBN 978-1-60684-162-4 (hardcover) — ISBN 978-1-60684-281-2
(electronic book) [1. Cryptography—Fiction. 2. Ciphers—Fiction.
3. Mystery and dectective stories.] I. Title.
PZ7.W2458Sec 2011
[Fic]—dc22
2011003240

Printed in the United States of America

CPSIA tracking label information:
Printed in July 2011 at Berryville Graphics, Berryville, Virginia

To my own Code Buster Club:
Luke Melvin, Lyla Melvin, Bradley Warner,
and Stephanie Warner.

READER

To see keys and solutions to the puzzles inside, go to the Code Buster's Key Book & Solutions on page 201.

To see complete Code Busters Club Rules and Dossiers, and solve more puzzles and mysteries, go to
www.CodeBustersClub.com

CODE BUSTERS CLUB RULES

Motto

To solve puzzles, codes, and mysteries and
keep the Code Busters Club secret!

Secret Sign

Interlocking index fingers
(American Sign Language sign for "friend")

Secret Password

Day of the week, said backward

Secret Meeting Place

Code Busters Club Clubhouse

Code Busters Club Dossiers

IDENTITY: Quinn Kee

Code Name: "Lock&Key"

Description
Hair: Black, spiky
Eyes: Brown
Other: Sunglasses

Special Skill: Video games, Computers, Guitar

Message Center: Doghouse

Career Plan: CIA cryptographer
or Game designer

Code Specialties: Military code,
Computer codes

IDENTITY: MariaElena—M.E.—Esperanto

Code Name: "Em-me"

Description
Hair: Long, brown
Eyes: Brown
Other: Fab clothes

Special Skill: Handwriting analysis, Fashionista

Message Center: Flower box

Career Plan: FBI handwriting analyst or Veterinarian

Code Specialties: Spanish, I.M., Text messaging

IDENTITY: Luke LaVeau

Code Name: "Kuel-Dude"

Description
Hair: Black, curly
Eyes: Dark brown
Other: Saints cap

Special Skill: Extreme sports, Skateboard, Crosswords

Message Center: Under step

Career Plan: Pro skater, Stuntman, Race car driver

Code Specialties: Word puzzles, Skater slang

IDENTITY: Dakota—Cody—Jones

Code Name: "CodeRed"

Description
Hair: Red, curly
Eyes: Green
Other: Freckles

Special Skill: Languages,
Reading faces and body language

Message Center: Tree knothole

Career Plan: Interpreter for UN or deaf people

Code Specialties: Sign language,
Braille, Morse code, Police codes

CONTENTS*

Chapter 1 1

Chapter 2 13

Chapter 3 21

Chapter 4 32

Chapter 5 44

Chapter 6 59

Chapter 7 66

Chapter 8 73

Chapter 9 80

Chapter 10

92

Chapter 11

109

Chapter 12

121

Chapter 13

135

Chapter 14

150

Chapter 15

161

Chapter 16

175

Chapter 17

192

Code Buster's Key Book & Solutions   201

*To crack the chapter title code, check out the CODE BUSTER'S Key Book & Solutions on pages 202 and 208.

Chapter 1

akota—Cody—Jones had just finished creating a puzzle for the Code Busters Club to decipher when she heard three quick taps on her upstairs bedroom window. She sat up at her desk and turned her head, listening intently.

Three more taps—this time spaced a beat apart.

Then three more quick taps, like the first three.

Cody darted to the window the minute she recognized the SOS call. In the dim light of the streetlamp, she spotted Quinn Key, a member of the Code Busters Club, clinging halfway up the giant ash tree by her window, his black spiky hair covered by a UC Berkeley baseball cap. The only thing missing were the sunglasses that he always wore.

He was holding a long stick.

Cody pulled up the window and stuck out her head. "Quinn, what are you doing?" she whispered. A breeze flipped the end of her red ponytail.

Quinn fumbled and dropped the stick. Cody watched it land several feet below.

"Quinn! Be careful!" Cody said.

"Come out!" he said. "I have to talk to you. It's important!" Cody held up a finger to show "one minute." She closed the window, put her hoodie on over her cat-decorated flannel pajamas, and tiptoed down the stairs. Her mother sat on the living room couch, riveted by an episode of *CSI*. Cody had no trouble slipping past her and out the front door.

"This better be important," Cody said to Quinn, crossing her arms to keep the fall chill out. "My mom will ground me until summer if she catches me out here. Or send me to jail." Cody's mother was a Berkeley, California, police officer, and Cody often teased her mom about locking Cody up in the local jail when she got into trouble.

"Look." Quinn nodded in the direction of the run-down Victorian opposite Cody's home. "Something weird is going on at Skeleton Man's house." Cody glanced across the street at the weed-infested yard and paint-chipped house, which was eerily lit by the soft glow of the streetlamp. "Looks the same to me," she said, shrugging. "Same weird sculptures in his yard. Same creepy junk on his porch. Same dirty curtains in the windows."

Quinn pointed to the second-floor window on the right. "Watch that window."

Cody gazed at Skeleton Man's tattered, yellowing curtain for a few seconds. A shadowy light glowed inside. "I don't see anything," she said, glancing back nervously at her front door. "My mom is—"

"Just wait!" Quinn whispered. He was staring up at the window as if expecting to see a ghost appear. "There! Did you see it?"

Cody gasped.

The curtain had fluttered.

A clawlike hand pulled the fabric back from the filthy, streaked window.

"So? He's looking out the window again. He's always doing that. You always say he spies on us, remember? But my mom said—"

Quinn cut her off. "Shh! Keep watching!"

Cody saw what looked like a bent, bony finger trace a line down the dirty glass pane. Another line appeared. Then another.

"Doesn't it look like he's writing something?" Quinn asked.

Cody strained in the semidarkness to see. "I guess so."

"I saw him drawing something on the window when I went outside to get my bike." Quinn lived on the other side of Skeleton Man and had been insisting for weeks that the old hermit was spying on them. Now he seemed to think that their neighbor was up to something else suspicious. But Quinn tended to see a mystery everywhere he looked.

In fact, that's why Quinn had started the Code Busters Club. During the first week at her new school, Cody had spotted a coded sign on one of the bulletin boards.

10-15-9-14 20-8-5 3-15-4-5 2-21-19-20-5-18-19 3-12-21-2

Ever since she'd learned sign language to

communicate with Tana, her deaf sister, she had loved being able to talk to people without others knowing what she was saying. Sign language was kind of like a code in that way. She'd quickly figured out that the message Quinn had written was in a math-based code called alphanumeric code. Each alphabet letter had been replaced by a number, beginning with A = 1, then B = 2, C = 3, and so on. To see what the message translates to, go to *Code Buster's Solution on p. 204.*

Being the new kid at Berkeley Cooperative Middle School, Cody had shown up hoping to make some friends. Quinn was the first person she had met, and they had hit it off immediately. She was especially excited to learn that he lived right across the street from her. He shared his code name with her—Lock&Key—and helped her make up her own: CodeRed, a combination of her name and her red hair. In the following weeks they had become great friends. When they weren't creating codes, they played puzzle-solving video games together with the other Code Buster members, M.E. and Luke. And Quinn was always coming up with something interesting to do, like now.

"Skeleton Man's never done that before," he continued, shaking his head. "Maybe he's trying to tell us something."

Cody squinted, trying to turn the lines into letters, but they didn't make sense. "They look more like drawings than letters. Stick figures," she said.

"Watch out!" Quinn grabbed her arm and pulled her to a squatting position beneath the big ash tree, nearly knocking her over. "Someone else is up there. Look!"

Cody saw the unfamiliar face of a woman at the window, peering out. She hoped she and Quinn hadn't been spotted—although they weren't doing anything wrong. Other than spying.

Moments later a puffy hand appeared at the window and swiped at the glass, blurring the carefully drawn lines. The curtains were suddenly jerked closed.

Cody looked at Quinn, who was scrunching up his nose. "That was weird."

"Seriously," Quinn said. "I thought Skeleton Man lived alone. Who was that person?"

Before Cody could answer, Skeleton Man's front door sprang open. She signaled Quinn to be quiet with a finger to her lips. A large woman with curly blonde hair, wearing a shapeless flowery dress, stepped onto the junk-filled porch. Frowning, she glanced around as if searching for something. Or someone?

Cody recognized her as the face at the upstairs window.

Seconds later, a short, skinny man squeezed out from behind the woman. Not Skeleton Man. The woman said something to the man, but Cody couldn't make out the words.

Quinn waved his hand forward—the military

signal for "move out." He was an expert at military codes and had taught the club members not only signals but military time codes.

Trying not to make noise, Cody and Quinn hunched down and scuttled to the curb, avoiding the streetlight beams. When they reached the street, they ducked behind Cody's mom's red Mini Cooper. Cody could hear the two people talking now.

"I *told* you to be careful, you old fart," the woman was saying. The man mumbled something just as a car drove by, muffling his words. Then the woman pointed toward Cody's house and said, "—sure I saw some kids over there..."

A chill ran down Cody's back. They'd been spotted! Suddenly, she felt hairs rubbing against her leg.

Punkin! One of Skeleton Man's many cats had seemingly adopted Cody and was now curling around her ankle. Cody loved cats, but she wasn't allowed to have pets because of her four-year-old sister's allergies. Still, that didn't stop her from pretending that the orange cat was hers. Yesterday she'd bought it a collar and had written the name "Punkin" on it in black marker. She stroked the cat while she strained to hear the two people talking on the porch.

"—we'll find it...got to be hidden around here somewhere...," the man said.

The large woman elbowed him sharply. "Shut up, you stupid old windbag! Somebody'll hear you. You wanna ruin everything we've worked for?" The woman squinted toward Cody's house, sending another shiver down Cody's spine.

"Dakota?" came a voice from behind her. It was her mom, calling from the front porch. "Are you out there?"

The sound of her mother's voice made the cat flee and Cody freeze. If she answered, she'd give away their hiding place, and those two weirdos across the street would know that kids *had* been spying on them. But if she didn't, she could be in real trouble with her police officer/mom.

"Cody! What are you doing behind my car?"

Too late. They'd been spotted. And those two weirdos across the street would know for sure they'd been spying on them.

"Come in here," her mother said. "It's a school night! You know you're not supposed to be out after dark." *Having a cop for a mom really has its disadvantages,* Cody thought, rising up from behind the car.

She glanced in the direction of Skeleton Man's porch, certain they'd also been discovered by the two strangers.

But the porch was empty.

She glanced up at the second-story window. It was dark.

"Coming, Mom," Cody called to her, then said to Quinn, "I've got to go. Set up a meeting with the Code Busters Club. There's something strange going on, that's for sure."

Quinn gave her a thumbs-up and headed home.

Cody headed inside, gave her mom a good-night hug, and got ready for bed, knowing there was no way she'd be getting any sleep tonight—not with Giant Flower Lady and her half-pint sidekick lurking around. She took a last glance out her window, looking for a sign of Skeleton Man or his visitors.

The house stood dark and the doorstep was empty.

The only movement was a flutter of the upstairs curtain.

Chapter 2

The screech of sirens woke Cody from a night-mare early the next morning, even before her alarm sounded. She'd been dreaming of mysterious symbols that she couldn't decode. She ran to the window. Although the sky was still dark, the whirling lights of two fire trucks lit up the street.

Skeleton Man's house was in flames!

Cody heard a loud rap on her bedroom door.

"Cody!" Her mom opened the door and peered in. "Good, you're up! Please wake your sister and get her dressed for preschool. I have to help out across the street." Her walkie-talkie squawked as she headed downstairs.

Because of her job, Cody's mother often got emergency calls in the middle of the night or early morning. When she had to leave on a moment's notice, she left Cody in charge of Tana until their dad could get there from his condo across town. It was just another complication After the Divorce. Cody's mom had taken the cop job in Berkeley and had moved the family there from Jamestown in the California Gold Country. Her dad, an attorney, had followed a month later to be closer to them.

Cody could barely tear herself away from the window. The billowing smoke and raging flames held her hypnotized. She watched as half a dozen firefighters leaped from the two trucks. Seconds later, forceful torrents of water arched over the roof, sending up more clouds of smoke into the semidark sky.

Spellbound, Cody saw a fireman ax his way through the front door. Smoke poured out of the house as he and two other firefighters in full protective gear—heavy-duty suits, helmets, face masks, gloves—disappeared inside. An ambulance sped up and four EMTs—emergency medical technicians—sprang out.

Cody spotted her mother down below, dressed in her navy-blue police uniform. She stood in the middle of the street directing traffic and ordering the gathering crowd of onlookers to keep back. Moments later the firefighters reappeared at the front door of Skeleton Man's house. One of them carried a slumped, pajama-clad body over his shoulder. The paramedics rushed over with their equipment, gently guided the man onto a stretcher, and placed an oxygen mask on his ashen face.

Skeleton Man.

Before Cody could tell whether he was still alive, the EMTs hoisted the gurney into the ambulance and sped off, sirens wailing and lights flashing. She felt a wave of sadness for the old man, a hermit hiding away in his own house. She wondered if any of the rumors about him were true…

Cody snapped out of her daze and ran to Tana's room.

She gave the little girl a gentle shake. "Wake up, Tana," she signed. Because Tana was deaf and couldn't hear the sirens, she had no clue what was going on outside. Cody signed to Tana using Finger spelling:

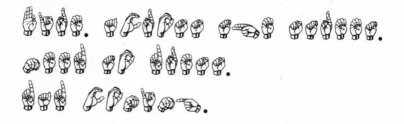

Code Buster's Key and Solution found on pp. 202, 204–205.

She helped Tana into a pink T-shirt and hoodie, blue overalls, and tennis shoes, then hurriedly dressed herself in jeans, a red T-shirt, and a matching hoodie. Taking Tana's hand, Cody led her down the stairs and out the front door for a closer look at the scene. She wasn't surprised to see Quinn standing in his front yard next door to the burning house, mesmerized by all the action.

The fire appeared to be nearly out by the time Cody reached the street. Still holding Tana's hand, she crossed over to Quinn's yard, where he stood with his parents, both math professors at UC Berkeley. Clumps of neighbors, once huddled together, now began returning to their homes.

"Any idea how the fire started?" Cody asked Quinn.

He shrugged. "No clue. I heard the sirens, saw the fire from my bedroom window. An ambulance came and took Skeleton Man..."

Cody frowned at the memory of the scene, then asked, "Hey, what about those other two people?"

"No sign of them," Quinn said.

Quinn's parents called to him as they headed back inside their house. He glanced at them, then back to Cody. "I've got to go. I'll set up a meeting with Luke and M.E. Check your secret hiding place later."

Cody nodded, spotting her mother walking toward them. She didn't look happy.

"Cody! Take Tana inside!" her mother said. "You two shouldn't be out here."

Cody nodded. As she crossed the street with Tana, she took a last look at Skeleton Man's blackened house. Suddenly, she caught a familiar face watching her from the sidelines.

Matt the Brat.

What was he doing all the way over on her street? Being nosy, of course. Her dad would have called him an ambulance chaser—always gawking at other people's troubles. Her mother had warned her to stay away from him. She'd been called to his house a couple of times—once because he threw a ball through a neighbor's window, again, and once because he was dumping trash cans in the neighborhood. But Cody couldn't avoid him— he sat right in front of her in class.

Some time later her father arrived early to take Tana to preschool. Cody greeted him with a hug and kiss and filled him in on the fire. When she realized it was time to get ready for school, she ran upstairs to get her backpack, but her head was still filled with questions. How had the fire started? Was Skeleton Man still alive? Who were those two mysterious people they'd seen at Skeleton Man's house last night?

And where were they now?

She paused, staring at the scorched house across the street. Glancing at the second-story window, she noticed the singed curtains lay still.

But she spotted something else that gave her goose bumps.

Clearly drawn on the windowpane in black marker were four stick figures.

Chapter 3

Cody stood on her front porch with her backpack, still shocked by the sight of the half-destroyed house across the street. Through the charred shell she could see that the fire had almost gutted the inside. A few firefighters still combed the area for smoldering ashes, and the air reeked of acrid smoke. Even the weedy yard had burned, leaving Skeleton Man's strange metal sculptures of trees and cats eerily discolored.

Cody had a sudden thought: Where was Punkin?

With the chaos of the fire, she'd forgotten all about the orange cat. She glanced over at Skeleton Man's singed yard for a sign of movement. The old man had more than a dozen cats—she'd actually counted them. Where were they now? And where was Punkin? What could have happened to him?

She checked her watch: 7:25 a.m. No time to search before school. M.E.—MariaElena, another member of the Code Busters Club—would be along any minute. Cody yawned. She'd been up for nearly two hours and was starting to feel the lack of sleep. With only a few minutes left before M.E. arrived, she walked over to her secret hiding place in the towering ash tree—the one Quinn had climbed the night before. Inside a knothole, in the secret spot where other Code Busters members knew to leave messages for her, she found a folded note.

Removing it, she studied the outside of the palm-sized message, which was addressed to her code name. A large orange dot, code for "Orange Alert," indicated its level of importance—the second highest just under "Red Alert." Cody unfolded the origami-style envelope. The discolored paper looked a hundred years old, with black smudges and ragged edges.

Almost as if it had been singed in a fire.

She glanced across at Skeleton Man's fire-scarred house and shuddered.

"Nice touch, Quinn," Cody said aloud, then looked around to see if anyone—like those two strangers from last night who had mysteriously appeared and then disappeared—had heard her.

Returning her attention to the note, she thought, *Leave it to Quinn to make it look super mysterious.* Quinn was gifted, thanks to his parents' super-genes. He had already designed computer games for the club, full of puzzles and codes, like Mutant

Zombies from the Cafeteria and Escape from Principal Grunt's Torture Chamber. And his coded messages were always fun to decipher. Although Quinn was on the shy side, he was full of creative ideas and was the unofficial leader of the club.

She smiled at the detail in his latest note. The paper had probably been soaked in tea, then wrinkled and darkened at the edges with dirt or ink to make it look really ancient. It reminded her of some of the old papers she'd seen during a school trip to the Gold Country Museum.

Before the Divorce.

That's how Cody saw life now. Before and After the Divorce.

A wave of longing for her old house and her old friends shot through her, creating a hole in her stomach. Moving to Berkeley—or Berzerkley, as her old friends in Jamestown had called it—had been a big change for her, After the Divorce. She remembered the day her mom and dad had called her into the living room and had told her that they would be living apart. Cody had barely heard the part where they had said the usual "reassuring things," like "We'll still be your parents" and "You didn't cause this." Blah, blah, blah.

Cody shook away her memories and studied the coded letters. She knew that if the note fell into the wrong hands—like Matt the Brat's, who was always snooping around—it wouldn't be easy to decipher. That's why all of the club's messages were written in code—so their secrets remained secret.

She leaned against the leafy tree. Checking her watch again, she wondered what was keeping M.E. Had she received a note, too?

Unlocking her Case Files Codebook with the key she always wore around her neck, Cody flipped to a blank page. She decided to work on Quinn's coded message until M.E. arrived.

Treating the codes like a math problem, Cody quickly recognized a pattern in this message. A smile spread across her face, creating dimples in her freckled cheeks. *Easy one*, she thought. It was based on the sequence of the alphabet. The Code Busters Club called it the **ABC code**.

"Ame bet cme dat eth fec glu hbh iou jse kaf lte mrs nch ooo pll qoc rka snd tke uyv wxyz."

Using her red pen, she crossed off the first letter in each group of letters, in sequence. Removing the "*a*" left "*m e*," the "*b*" left "*e t*," the "*c*" left "*m e*," and so on. When she was finished, she scanned the note again. The last several letters—*vwxyz*—she knew were just leftovers. She drew a line through them and looked over the letters that remained.

"me et me at th ec lu bh ou se af te rs ch oo ll oc ka nd ke y"

26

She rewrote the letters, fixed the spacing, and added punctuation.

Code Buster's Solution found on p. 205.

Cody refolded the note. She already knew Quinn had planned to call a meeting, but had he learned something more about the fire—or those two strange people at Skeleton Man's house?

She looked up at the odd drawings on Skeleton Man's window. Turning to a fresh page, she quickly copied them down to show the other club members. They seemed like stick figures standing in different positions.

"Dakota Jones!" her mother called from the front porch. "Get going! You're going to be late for school again!" Her dad was getting ready to leave so he could drop off Tana before he went to the law firm where he worked.

Startled, Cody closed her notebook and moved to the sidewalk. "I'm still waiting for M.E.," she called back. Her mother stood at the front door, one hand hooked in her leather belt, the other over her gun holster. Cody's sister Tana stood next to her, a miniature carbon copy of her mother. Both were blonde, blue-eyed, and sturdy. Cody had inherited her father Mike's genes—his fiery red hair (a constant source of teasing), green eyes, and slim form. And freckles.

Cody waved to Tana as she and her dad headed for his car. Their mom was walking toward her Mini Cooper.

Tana signed, "Bye bye," to Cody through the car's side window. Cody signed back, "I love you," holding up the shortcut sign—the American Sign Language (called ASL) letters *I*, *L*, and *Y* combined. It was their morning good-bye ritual.

"Get to school," Cody's mom called out. "And be careful." The daily warning had become her mother's good-bye ritual.

As they all drove off, Cody gazed across the street, hoping to spot Punkin. There didn't appear to be any life in Skeleton Man's yard. Where had all his cats gone? And who would feed them when they came back, now that Skeleton Man was…

"Hey, Cody!" a high-pitched voice called from down the street.

At last! Cody spotted M.E.—MariaElena Esperanto—running to meet her, her long dark hair swaying as she walked. She grinned at her friend's glittering pants, purple peasant top, SpongeBob cartoon knee-highs, and black hiking boots. M.E. always wore creative outfits. She lived with her big family one street over—where she spoke mostly Spanish—and had met Quinn and Luke in a summer camp called Cryptology for Kids. They'd been great friends ever since.

M.E. gawked at the house across the street, her mouth wide open at the sight. "Oh no! I heard the sirens and smelled the smoke, but my parents wouldn't let me check it out. What happened to Skeleton Man's house?"

"It caught on fire early this morning," Cody said. "The paramedics took him to the hospital in an ambulance."

"Wow. Is he...all right?" M.E. asked.

"I don't know. I'm sure my mom will find out."

M.E. spun her lettered Code Bracelet around her latte-colored wrist as she stared at the burned-out house. It was her habit when she was nervous or worried. Cody wore a bracelet just like it. They'd made the bracelets together—following the instructions on an Internet site—by stringing lettered beads onto elastic thread. When they wanted to send each other secret messages, they wrote down numbers on a piece of paper using the Caesar cipher—a decoder wheel—where each letter of the alphabet correlates to a number. Then they'd translate the code by matching the numbers to the correct letters.

"Did you get a secret message from Quinn?" Cody asked.

"Yeah," M.E. said, snapping out of her trance.

"What's it mean? Something to do with the fire?"

"Maybe more," Cody answered. As they began the five-block trek to Berkeley Cooperative Middle School, Cody filled M.E. in on the events of last night—Quinn's Morse code tap, the mysterious drawings on Skeleton Man's window, the two strangers and their odd disappearance after the fire.

"Weird," M.E. said.

Cody looked at her friend, puzzled at her quiet demeanor. Usually M.E. was full of energy and talking a mile a minute, sometimes breaking into Spanish and losing Cody entirely. "What's wrong?"

"Nothing," M.E. said, sighing. "I'm just a little bummed. When I heard the sirens this morning, I thought maybe the school was burning down—I'm not ready for the test in social studies today. But no such luck."

Maybe not lucky for M.E., but definitely not lucky for Skeleton Man, Cody thought.

Or had the fire really been *just* bad luck?

Chapter 4

Cody and M.E. arrived at school just in time for the first bell. By the second bell—the "late bell"—Cody was in her seat behind Matt the Brat, studying the stick figure sketches she'd copied into her Case Files Codebook earlier that morning. The first figure held its right arm out to the side, the left across its chest and down at a forty-five-degree angle. The second figure held its right arm straight down, the left up and out. The third's right arm was pointing down at an angle, and the left pointed up at the opposite angle. The fourth one held a right hand straight out and the left one straight up.

What did the figures mean? Was Skeleton Man sending some sort of message? Why had someone tried to wipe them off the windowpane?

And what was up with those two creepy people?

"Dakota Jones?"

Ms. Stadelhofer's husky voice startled Cody from her thoughts. Her teacher's bushy brown hair bounced as she shook her head in irritation. Stad was a pretty cool teacher most of the time, even though she always wore a ridiculous themed vest with her outfits. Today's vest featured apples, rulers, and miniature blackboards—the classic schoolteacher theme.

"Uh, here!" Cody said a little too loudly as her

hand shot into the air. Everyone in class turned to her and giggled. She felt her face flush, certain she was lit up like a freckled fireball.

She scrunched down in her seat and looked out the window, her swinging ponytail tickling her back. As the teacher finished calling roll, Cody returned to her daydream about the stick figures, mulling over the positions of their arms, but when Stad's vocab lesson began, Cody tuned back in to the classwork.

Cody didn't mind school. That's because she viewed each subject as a puzzle to solve. To her, spelling was just coded letters, and math was coded numbers. Even social studies was full of mysteries to be solved—puzzling sphinxes, lost civilizations, and mysterious dinosaur disappearances. But she'd never let the other kids know she liked school. Not cool.

"Hey, dipwad," said Matt the Brat, twisting around in his chair. Matt was a wannabe skater and wore the outfits to match. Trouble was, he didn't know *how* to skateboard. Today he had on a skull T-shirt, baggy jeans, and ginormous, multicolored athletic shoes, worn without laces. His breath reeked of peanut butter—he was always eating the stuff straight from a jar he kept in his backpack. He would have had nice eyes if he wasn't always using them to spy on people.

When Cody didn't answer, Matt looked down at her vocab paper. "Writing another one of your *secret* messages?" he asked.

Cody had quickly learned that Matt was a bully. He liked to pick on the new kids at school. He had been held back a year, making him bigger than the other seventh graders. Sometimes she caught him staring out the window, and she wondered where he'd gone in his mind. She felt sorry for him, knowing how hard it must have been for him to see his friends move on. But he was always in her face—with that peanut-butter breath. And always snooping around the Code Busters Clubhouse and making fun of them. Her mom had said his behavior had to do with his home life, but since he sat in front of Cody in class, thanks to their last names—Jeffreys and Jones—Cody had to deal with his school life.

Before she could pull her paper away, Matt scribbled an ugly monster over her vocab words. He wasn't half bad when it came to drawing monsters, but she didn't appreciate it when he defaced her work. She jerked the paper away, tearing a hole in the middle of it in the process. *Great*, she thought. *Now I'll have to recopy the whole paper.* Matt laugh-snorted, leaned sideways in his chair, and lifted one leg.

Oh no, no, no. The Silent but Deadly.

The smell nearly knocked her out of her seat. She tried to fan it away. She held her breath to concentrate on rewriting her vocab list, but it was nearly impossible. The school day had barely started, and already she felt as if it would never end.

Halfway through first period, Lyla, the girl who sat behind Cody, tapped her on the back. When she turned, Lyla handed her a folded note. Slipping her arm across her chest and her hand behind her back, she took the folded message, then tucked it under her math homework.

"Dakota Jones! Is that a note?" Cody looked up to see Stad frowning at her.

She froze.

Busted!

"No, Sta— Uh, Ms. Stadelhofer. I...was just going over my math homework. See?" Cody held up the homework sheet with one hand, covering the note with her other hand.

"Well, put it away. It's not math time yet," Ms. Stadelhofer said before continuing her lecture. Matt the Brat turned around, smirking.

"Matthew Jeffreys, turn around or it's the principal's office for you," Ms. Stadelhofer threatened.

Matt stuck his tongue out of the side of his mouth to Cody before turning back.

Cody let out a breath.

Close one.

When she was sure Stad was no longer watching, she quietly unfolded the note. It was written in Caesar's cipher, decipherable only if you had the corresponding decoder wheel.

3-2-12-8 21-2-9-22-4-8 8-2 15-4-4-8 15-4 16-8
8-19-4 21-13-16-22-23-2-13-4 16-21-8-4-9 7-1-19-2-2-13

15.4.

She checked the clock again. Only a few seconds to decipher the note before the bell rang. Pulling out her decoder wheel from another compartment of her backpack, she slid the dial around to each of the numbers and jotted down the corresponding letters underneath.

It took only seconds to translate the code.

Code Buster's Key and Solution found on pp. 203, 205.

The bell rang.

"Yooou got in trou-ble," said Matt the Brat in a singsong voice as he grinned broadly. He stood up, blocking her way down the aisle with his bulk.

"No, I didn't." Cody hoisted on her backpack, then swung around, bumping Matt out of the way.

Ms. Stad looked up from the pile of spelling papers on her desk. She eyed Cody. Before Cody could escape, the room filled with the familiar sound of static on the loudspeaker. It was the deep gravelly voice of Principal Grunt.

"Attention, students! This is Principal Grant speaking. I don't want to alarm you, but we've received a notice from the Berkeley Police Department that a mountain lion has been sighted in the hills near the campus."

Several students gasped.

"There's no need to panic, but stay alert, and away from the hills until further notice. Thank you, and have a pleasant afternoon. Go Eagles."

Cody rolled her eyes. *That's all I need*, she thought. *First a fire. Then Matt the Brat. And now a mountain lion on the loose.*

Could it get any worse?

The rest of the day passed as slowly as first period had. When the final bell rang at the end of school, Cody raced to join M.E. at the flagpole, their usual meeting place. Her friend looked as sparkly and as radiant as she had that morning.

"I thought this day would never end," Cody said to M.E. as she scanned the mass of kids pouring from the school building. There was no sign of Matt the Brat, but that didn't mean he wasn't nearby. Probably spying on her and planning his next prank.

"Totally," M.E. said.

Cody glanced around. "Careful. I might have been followed," she whispered as they headed off campus.

M.E.'s dark eyes flashed. "Matt the Brat?"

Cody nodded.

"He likes you, you know. That's why he's always bugging you." M.E. glanced sideways at her.

"How do you know?" Cody scrunched up her face in disgust.

"I saw it on a TV show. This guy was always teasing this girl, and she couldn't stand him. But then she found out he really liked her and so she started being nicer to him, and he quit bugging her..."

Cody half listened as she glanced around for a glimpse of Matt's X-Men cap or skull-emblazoned T-shirt. There was no way Matt liked her—not the way he acted. At least, Cody hoped not.

"So maybe you should ask him out!" M.E. said, giggling.

"Shut up!" Cody gave her a death look, then

checked her watch. "Come on. Let's get to the club-house before he follows us."

The two girls sprinted to the end of the block. Just as they started up the hill toward the euca-lyptus forest, M.E. suddenly stopped and grabbed Cody's arm.

"What about the mountain lion?" she asked, her eyes wide. "Grunt said it was in these hills."

"Don't worry," Cody said. "There were tons of mountain lions where I used to live. They usually hunt at night, not daytime. My teacher told us if you see one, don't run. Just make some noise. And try to look bigger."

M.E. stared up at Cody, who towered over her by at least six inches. "Oh yeah? How am I sup-posed to look bigger?"

Cody grinned, then flapped her arms up and down. "Wave your arms like this. Come on. We'll be safe in the clubhouse."

As soon as the words were out of her mouth,

Cody heard a crunchy noise coming from a nearby bush.

She looked at M.E. to see if she'd heard the sound, too.

M.E. stood like a statue, her eyes as wide as her open mouth. "What was that?" she whispered.

"I don't know, but let's get out of here!"

In spite of everything they'd been told, they ran.

Chapter 5

By the time the girls reached the clubhouse, they were out of breath and their hearts were racing like frightened cats.

"We made it!" M.E. wheezed.

Cody panted from the uphill run, nearly the length of two football fields. "No sign of the mountain lion," she gasped, glancing behind her to make sure. "But something was in those bushes."

The clubhouse stood hidden in the middle of a eucalyptus forest. Cody loved it here, where the city seemed miles away. This peaceful, wooded hillside reminded her of her home in the Gold Country. It smelled like the Vicks VapoRub that her mom used to spread on her chest when she had a cold. Eucalyptus.

The boys, Quinn and Luke, had begun building the clubhouse a year ago, using old billboard panels as walls, propped up and tied with rope between four trees. Quinn had designed the structure, while Luke, already muscular from doing extreme sports, did most of the heavy lifting. Piece by piece, they had added on to the clubhouse with materials they'd found discarded around town. They had covered the top with an old camo parachute and had painted the outside walls green and brown to blend in with the surroundings. To someone passing by the forest, it would be almost invisible. The dirt floor was covered with a piece of sheet metal they'd found abandoned at a construction site.

Once it was finished, they'd secured it with a chain and combination lock. After recruiting M.E., then Cody, they'd moved the Code Busters Club inside and loaded the place with secondhand spy supplies, secret notebooks, and packaged food for emergencies.

Quinn, a military fanatic, had brought some cool night-vision binoculars he'd found at a garage sale, plus a broken code breaking machine (missing three keys). Luke, influenced by his grandmother's crossword puzzle hobby, contributed several codebooks he'd discovered in her attic, including one that featured Civil War codes and one about the Navajo code talkers.

M.E. had made Code Bracelets for everyone, but only Cody and M.E. wore them. The boys kept them in their pockets. And Cody had brought four multipocketed vests she'd found. They had room to store secret messages, notebooks, and other confidential stuff. M.E. had decorated them with the club initials in sign language: 🖐️🤟🖐️.

They kept their important collection—along with flashlights, compasses, sign language books, and other club valuables—stashed in a pit they'd dug in the ground and covered with the metal flooring.

Cody turned the combination lock to the first number, then froze. "Shhh!" she hissed at M.E. "I hear something!"

M.E. grabbed Cody's hand. "What is it?" she whispered.

Cody stared through the dense forest behind her. While the day was bright and cheery, the forest was always filled with dark shadows. "I think someone...or something...is out there."

"You think Matt followed us?" M.E. asked,

moving closer to Cody and gazing at the tall, fragrant trees.

Cody didn't answer. Instead, she finished turning the combination lock, removed it, and tried to push open the door. It wouldn't give. Someone had bolted it from the inside. She pounded on the clubhouse door, then abruptly stopped. She'd forgotten to give the secret knock, her initials in Morse code. Realizing this, she took a deep breath and tapped out the code:

One tap, a pause, two quick taps, a double pause, a quick tap, a tap, a pause, a tap, a pause, a tap.

- .. .- - -

Code Buster's Key and Solution found on pp. 202, 205.

Next she whispered the day's secret password through the eyehole in the plywood door: ***"Yadsendew."***

The password changed every day of the week, making it hard for spies to fake their way in. But it was easy for the Code Busters to remember. You just had to know the day of the week—and how to say it backward. Today was Wednesday, so the password was Wednesday, said backward: **yadsendew**.

Cody heard the heavy metal bar scraping against the inside of the door as it was lifted. The door jerked open, revealing Quinn, wearing the sleek aviator sunglasses he'd found on eBay.

"Hurry!" M.E. squealed, pushing Cody forward. Meanwhile, Quinn grabbed Cody by the arm and pulled her through the narrow opening, then did the same to M.E.

"What's wrong? Were you followed?" Quinn asked, peeking outside.

"Shut the door!" M.E. said.

But before Quinn could close it, a voice called out from down the hill. "Dude, wait up!"

Cody breathed a sigh of relief. "Thank goodness! It's only Luke." She smiled, dropping to the floor and rubbing her tired legs as the fourth and final member of the Code Busters Club emerged from the shadows.

As Luke LaVeau reached the clubhouse, Quinn widened the door to let him inside. The tallest in the group, Luke had to duck to enter, knocking his New Orleans Saints cap off. He pulled the door shut behind him, set down the metal bar, then looked at Cody and smiled shyly.

Cody felt herself blush and hoped the others didn't notice. She'd never admit it to anyone, but she had a little crush on Luke, with his curly black hair, mocha skin, liquid brown eyes, and super-broad shoulders. She also liked that, although he seemed fearless, he acted a little shy around her. She loved the way he said certain words, like "Y'all" instead of "You guys," and "N'awlins" instead of "New Orleans," in his southern accent. He was born in Louisiana. But his parents had died in the flooding after Hurricane Katrina, and he and his grandmother, whom he called Grand-mère, ended up living in Berkeley together.

"Sorry I'm late," Luke said, setting down his battered, decal-decorated skateboard and retrieving his cap. "I heard something in the bushes and went to check it out. Thought it might be that mountain lion the principal told us about. But I didn't see anything."

"You didn't actually go *looking* for the mountain lion, did you?" Cody asked. "That's just plain crazy. What if it really had been the lion?"

Luke and the others joined Cody, sitting cross-legged on the metal floor. There was just enough room in the cozy clubhouse to fit them all comfortably.

"I was careful," Luke said, shrugging.

Cody shook her head.

"So what's up, Quinn?" M.E. asked, pulling out the note she'd received from him that morning. "Your message was Code Orange."

Quinn took off his sunglasses and looked at each of them before speaking, as if building up the suspense. He took a deep breath and began. "Okay. You know the fire at Skeleton Man's house?"

"Yeah," M.E. said. Luke and Cody nodded.

"Last night," Quinn continued, "before the fire, Cody and I saw these two weird people at his house." He told the story of the mysterious activities he and Cody had witnessed the previous night—the drawings on the window, the face behind the curtain, the two strangers talking on the porch, the rescue of Skeleton Man, and the sudden disappearance of the man and woman after the fire.

"Weird," M.E. said, rubbing the goose bumps on her arm. "Skeleton Man totally creeps me out— and now he's got two creepy friends?"

"He creeps me out, too," Quinn said. "And I live next door to him. One time when I was in the backyard, he started shouting at me from his window. I couldn't understand a word he said. He's always spying on us."

"Plus I heard his house is haunted," M.E. added. "And this kid I know said he buries his cats in his yard when they die. He's got, like, fifty of them."

Cody shook her head at the silly rumors. "I don't believe in haunted houses or cat graveyards or ghosts. Besides, he takes good care of his animals. I've watched him feed his cats and work on his lawn sculptures. He's just old. I feel sorry for him."

"I don't know anything about his house being haunted," Quinn continued, "but I think those two weirdos were up to something. Cody and I overheard them talking about a treasure."

"Treasure?" Luke looked up from studying his athletic shoes. His dark eyes gleamed.

Quinn shrugged. "Yeah, but then the house suddenly caught on fire and—"

"You think those two people started it?" M.E. interrupted, her eyes wide.

"No clue," Quinn said. "But they were definitely snooping around. Maybe they were looking for that treasure. I heard Skeleton Man used to be a gold prospector."

"Wow!" Luke said. "You think there's gold hidden on his property?"

"And dead cats?" M.E. added.

Quinn shrugged. "Very funny, M.E." He looked at the others, one eyebrow raised.

"Maybe we should go find out," Cody offered.

Before anyone could say anything more, a loud boom shook one wall of the clubhouse.

"Mountain lion!" M.E. screamed, grabbing Cody and hugging her tightly.

Luke leaped up and peered through the eyehole in the door, while the others sat frozen to their spots. Cody could hear her heartbeat through her T-shirt and wondered if everyone else could hear it, too.

After a few tense seconds, Luke whispered, "I don't see anything."

"Well, something hit the wall!" M.E. said. "Either that or the clubhouse is haunted, too."

Luke unbolted the door and cracked it open a foot. He stuck his head out, looked around, then took a step outside, searching for any sign of movement.

Cody thought, *He's so brave.* She rose and followed him to the door, but remained inside.

Moving around to the side, Luke called out, "I think I see something...."

He was quiet for so long, Cody finally said, "Is it the mountain lion?"

"I don't think so. Unless it's wearing a T-shirt. Whoever it was, he's disappeared behind the trees."

Probably Matt the Brat, Cody thought, stepping outside. Quinn rose, put on his sunglasses, and followed her. Then came a reluctant M.E.

"Let's get out of here!" M.E.'s voice quavered. Cody could see that her friend was terrified.

"You're safer inside the clubhouse," Quinn said. "Stay here. I'll go check it out with Luke." Cody and M.E. huddled in the doorway.

Luke had disappeared from sight behind the clubhouse. Cody waited, barely breathing, squeezing M.E.'s hand. Seconds later she heard Luke call out from the back of the clubhouse, "You can come out now."

Cody and M.E. followed Quinn's route around to the back of the clubhouse, where they found Luke holding a rounded stone the size of a softball.

"Well, that was no mountain lion. Unless mountain lions can throw rocks."

Cody looked at the clubhouse wall and spotted a dent in the siding.

Luke held up the stone for the others to see. It was wrapped in a piece of paper secured with a rubber band.

He removed the rubber band and unwrapped the paper. Letters of various sizes cut from a magazine or newspapers had been glued to the paper. Luke read the note aloud.

KEEP AWAY FROM MY HOUSE SKELLETON MAN

Cody took the note from Luke, looked it over, and gave a short laugh. "This is so bogus. Whoever wrote this spelled *Skeleton* wrong. And besides, how could Skeleton Man write this anyway? He's in the hospital. It's totally fake."

"Yeah, but whoever it is obviously knows his nickname," Luke added. "Someone's trying to scare us away from his place."

"But why?" Cody asked.

"And who else knows his nickname?" M.E. asked.

"Lots of kids in the neighborhood do, and our parents know we call him that," Quinn said. "But something's up. And I think we should go over there and find out."

Chapter 6

After dinner with her mother and Tana, Cody went outside to search in her front yard again for her adopted cat. She checked some bushes and behind her ash tree, then called across the street, "Punkin! Here, kitty, kitty!" Still no sign of the orange tabby. Cody hoped he—she?—was just hiding somewhere safe and would turn up soon.

Remembering Quinn's plan to contact the club members, she looked inside the knothole of the ash tree as she passed by. Nothing. Maybe Quinn had texted her. She headed inside and climbed the stairs to her bedroom to check her cell phone. Two messages were waiting. She sat on her bed to read them.

SUP Red.
GL on SP test.
YGG. TTYL.
POP. (((H)))

Her dad was so funny, trying to sound cool when he texted her. It always made her laugh.

Hi Pop.
THNX.
CUL8R.
(Red)

Code Buster's Solution found on p. 206.

The next message was not as clear.

MTTTHLBRRYT 1900HRS

Cody recognized the consonant code. It was a message composed of words that were all run together, minus the vowels. When she first read it aloud, it sounded like mumbo jumbo. But after repeating the syllables a few times, Cody began to hear familiar words. She wrote down her best guesses in her Case Files Codebook. "MT" became "meet," "T" had to be "at," "TH" was obviously "the," and so on.

Code Buster's Solution found on p. 206.

As usual, Quinn had used the military time code for the meeting time. Nineteen hundred hours meant 7:00 p.m.

Cody checked her watch. *That was in fifteen minutes!*

She quickly texted him back:

CN I RIDE W/ U?

Seconds later, a letter popped up: **Y**

Since the September nights were cooling off, Cody changed out of her shorts and tank top. She searched her room for something to wear, but the piles of clothes strewn over her bed and floor didn't make it easy. After digging through the cloth- ing, she found her favorite jeans and red hoodie, slipped them on, and gathered her backpack. She headed downstairs to get her mom's permission.

Of course, Cody couldn't tell her mother the real reason she wanted to go to the library: to meet with the Code Busters Club and make plans to look for Skeleton Man's treasure—if there was one. She'd have to come up with a good reason for going out on a school night. As usual, she found her mom on the cushy couch watching another rerun of *CSI*.

She was wearing her blue sweats, her hair in a twist, and was eating carrot sticks dipped in hummus. *How can she eat that stuff?* Cody thought. Her mom had really gone Berzerkley since they'd moved here.

"Mom, I need to go to the library. Just for an hour, okay?" Cody tried to sound casual.

"It's a school night," her mother said, glancing over at Cody. "You have homework."

"I'm working on a project with Quinn." She wasn't exactly lying. She just wasn't overexplaining.

Her mother glanced at the clock. "It's almost seven."

"I'll be home by eight. Promise."

"Okay, but I can't take you. Tana's in bed, and you can't walk there at this time of night."

"Quinn's mom is driving. They're picking me up in a few minutes."

Her mom sighed in defeat. "Okay, but take your

cell phone and call when you get there. *And* when you leave the library."

Her mother, being a cop, had seen a lot of bad stuff on the job, but Cody wished she would relax a little. Cody could take care of herself. She'd learned that After the Divorce.

Checking to make sure her Case Files Codebook was in her backpack, she stood at the front window and watched for Quinn's SUV to back out of his driveway.

Cody headed for the front door. "Bye, Mom!" she called out.

"Got your spelling list?" her mom asked, eyeing her suspiciously.

"Right here." Cody tapped her backpack. "Quinn will test me."

Cody didn't really need to be quizzed on her words. Learning to spell was like deciphering a code. Some words were phonetic, like "man-da-tor-y" or "as-ton-ish." All she had to do was sound

64

out each syllable. Some she broke into separate smaller words, like "book-worm" or "sleep-less." If the word had a silent letter, she'd pronounce it, as if speaking a new language, like "ga-nat" for "gnat" and "ni-ece" for "niece." And if it was a really hard word, such as "vacuum," she'd create an acronym for the letters: "Vicky ate cookies under Utah mountains." She almost always got 100 percent.

Just to make sure, she'd look over her new words at the library—twice—and again later that night when she was in bed. But first, there was the matter of supposedly hidden money in a supposedly haunted house where a supposedly crazy man lived.

And that note warning them to stay away.

Chapter 7

The neighborhood branch of the Berkeley Community Library looked like a Gothic castle that should have held ghosts and spirits rather than books and magazines. According to a sign by the heavy front doors, the three-story structure was more than a hundred years old. Cody loved the place, especially the maze of musty rooms, crowded shelves, and hidden stacks that spread throughout the building.

The Code Busters often met at the library after school, to do their homework and research codes. Each time they met at a different location there. The first person to arrive wrote a math code, signed it "Dewey," and stuck it on the library bulletin board. The rest of the Code Busters had to solve the code—based on the Dewey Decimal System—to determine their meeting place. Once the kids had the correct answer, they knew where to go.

Quinn led the way to the bulletin board and quickly spotted the message. It read: "Math Question of the Day: $5 \times 5 + 6 \times 6 + 9 \times 9 + 400 - 37 =$???"

Code Buster's Solution found on p. 206.

"Easy one," Quinn said. "It's on the second floor." Cody followed him up the stairs and through a labyrinth of bookshelves until they reached the right row. At the end of the row they found Luke at a small table reading a copy of *Goofyfoot*, his favorite skateboarding magazine. He often talked about becoming a professional skater—or a stunt-man. Cody had no doubt he would succeed at either one. Luke was strong, athletic, and fearless. He looked up and grinned at Cody.

"Hey," he said, rolling up the magazine. "About time."

Cody smiled back. She felt her cheeks burning.

Quinn, oblivious to the interaction between Cody and Luke, glanced around to make sure the area was clear of any potential spies. Once he determined the coast was clear, he plopped into a stiff wooden chair.

Cody slid into the chair next to Quinn, opposite Luke, and opened her backpack. She pulled out her spelling words along with her Case Files Codebook, figuring she'd study a little until M.E. arrived and the meeting officially started. But before she could look at the first word on the list, her friend appeared from the stacks.

"Hey, guys," M.E. said, sitting next to Luke. She'd exchanged her school outfit for blue overalls, a stretchy pink top studded with rhinestones, and pink bunny slippers. There was nothing M.E. wouldn't wear—including pajama bottoms. Cody often wished she had the nerve to dress like M.E., but it just wasn't her style.

Before officially beginning the meeting, the Code Busters gave the secret greeting: they each made a fist and touched their thumbnails to their lips— the American Sign Language sign for "secret."

"'Sup, dude?" Luke asked Quinn, apparently eager to get the meeting started. *A man of action,* Cody thought.

Quinn leaned in and spoke in a hushed voice. "Okay, first we need a plan to find the treasure at Skeleton Man's house."

"How do you know there really is a treasure?"

M.E. asked, twisting her long black hair up with a scrunchy. "If he's so rich, why hasn't he fixed up his house or built a swimming pool or bought a race car or something?"

"Because he's crazy," Quinn said, tapping his forehead. "I mean, he has all those weird statues in his yard. And, like, a hundred cats."

Cody rolled her eyes at the common rumor about Skeleton Man's so-called menagerie. "No, he doesn't. I told you. He only has *eleven.* I counted them once." She thought about Punkin and bit her lip. Where was *her* cat?

"But what's going to happen to them with Skeleton Man gone?" M.E. asked. M.E.'s bedroom was like a mini-zoo. She had a bird, a guinea pig, a white rat, and a turtle. Cody envied her, but with Tana's allergies, about all she could own was a turtle.

"My mom called the SPCA," Quinn said. "They're going to come and get the cats."

Not Punkin! Cody thought. *They can't take my cat away!*

"What's SPCA?" Luke asked. "Some kind of code?"

"An acronym, doofus," M.E. said. "The letters stand for Society for the Prevention of Cruelty to Animals. They take care of sick and abandoned cats and dogs."

"That's cool," Luke said. "I had a dog, back in N'awlins…" He drifted off without finishing his sentence. Cody wondered if the dog had been lost in the flood.

"Anyway," Quinn interrupted, "back to the plan. You know those two strangers who were over at Skeleton Man's house? My mom talked to them and found out they're his relatives. At least, that's what they said."

"She talked to them?" Luke asked, raising his eyebrows.

"Yeah, when she saw them hanging around after

71

the fire, she went over to ask about Skeleton Man."

"Wait a minute. Those two were at his house—*after* the fire?" Cody hadn't seen them and thought that they were gone by the time the house was in flames. "What else did they say?"

"They told my mom they didn't know anything yet about how Skeleton Man was doing," Quinn said. "Which was kinda weird, if they were relatives. But then they changed the subject and started asking my mom a bunch of questions."

"Like wh—" Cody said.

Before she could finish her question, she glimpsed a shadow moving behind one of the magazine racks. She held up her hand—the scuba diving sign for "stop!" Then she finger-spelled the letters "s-p-y" and pointed in the direction of the movement.

Someone was lurking in the stacks—and listening in.

Chapter 8

Cody eased out of her chair and moved as stealthily as a mountain lion to the magazine rack. After taking a breath, she peered over the top.

An older woman stood leafing through a book on Berkeley architecture.

She breathed a sigh of relief. Her imagination was working overtime.

With a last glance around, she returned to the table. She motioned the others to keep their voices down.

"So…what did your mom find out, Quinn?" M.E. whispered.

"Well, the big woman asked if Mom knew anything about a will," Quinn said.

M.E. blinked. "What did she say?"

Quinn shook his head. "She told her no, but she thought it was a weird question for relatives to ask."

Luke sat up. "Then there must be a will."

Cody nodded, then checked her watch and quickly gathered her things. "I have to get back, Quinn. My mom will kill me if I'm late. Let's find your mom."

"Wait, we haven't made a plan yet," Quinn said. "If Luke's right, if there *is* a will, maybe it's hidden in a safe somewhere in his house. Maybe there's cash, too, or something valuable. He used to be a gold prospector, remember? Maybe he has a pile of gold buried in the backyard or hidden in the attic...or in the basement. I think that's why those two snoops suddenly showed up—to find his treasure."

"It is kind of weird that the house suddenly caught on fire after the cousins arrived," Luke added, putting the word *cousins* in finger quotes. "I say we check it out."

"I agree," Quinn said. "Let's find whatever it is, before those guys do!"

M.E. frowned. "Like, how are we going to do that? There's no way I'm going to snoop around a burned-up haunted house at night. First of all, it's dark out, so we wouldn't find anything without some light. Second, if I get caught sneaking out, I'll be grounded until I graduate. And third, we don't even know if there *is* anything to find."

Quinn hushed her and looked around to see if anyone had overheard M.E.'s rant. Just in case someone was listening in, he said the key words in double Dutch. "Nag-ot to-nag-ite. To-mag-or-rag-ow."

Code Buster's Solution found on p. 206.

M.E. shrugged. "But even if we find something, it's not ours. So what's the point? Besides, it's dangerous. The roof might cave in on us. We might get trapped. The fire might start up again."

Cody knew M.E. was not the bravest girl on the planet. But she had a point—in fact, several points. They needed to make sure the place was safe enough to explore before they went snooping around inside.

"It's not going to cave in," Quinn insisted. "I heard the fire marshal say that to the TV reporter. But even if it does cave in, we'll *all* be there to help each other. And it's not going to catch on fire again, 'cause it's totally water-soaked."

Cody spoke up. "I suppose if we found anything, we could make sure it gets back to Skeleton Man and not those creepy so-called relatives of his."

"And we might get a reward," Luke added. "Then we could really fix up the clubhouse, buy some walkie-talkies, get some of those listening devices...."

M.E. brightened. "I know! If we find the money, we could use it to save his cats. We could help build a cat sanctuary."

"Great idea!" Cody said, thinking about Punkin. She high-fived M.E.

M.E.'s enthusiasm suddenly dimmed. "It could still be dangerous. What about that note we found, warning us to stay off his property?"

"It was probably from Matt the Brat," Luke said. "I'll bet he followed us to the clubhouse and was listening in. I'm pretty sure it was his skull T-shirt I saw in the trees. He's just trying to scare us off."

Cody smiled at Luke, then M.E. and Quinn. "Okay, I'm in."

"Me, too." Luke stuck out his fist.

M.E. shrugged and met his fist. Quinn and Cody followed.

Cody checked her watch again and stood. "I've really got to go, or I'll never be let out again. My mom will lock me up and throw away the key, without a chance for parole, even with my dad defending me. So…what time tomorrow? After school?"

"No, not in broad daylight," Quinn said. "I was thinking oh–six hundred tomorrow morning. There won't be many people up at that hour to see us. And we'll have plenty of time before school starts."

As the Code Busters Club gang headed for the stairs, Cody took one last look around, remembering that woman reading the book about Berkeley, but she saw nothing but shadows. Pushing through the heavy front door, Cody bumped into a large woman in a flowery dress. The crash caused the woman to drop an armload of books.

"Watch it, kid!" the woman snapped at Cody. She spun around and glared at the small man behind her. He quickly knelt down and gathered up the tumbled books.

Cody was about to apologize when Quinn grabbed her arm and pulled her outside. She jerked her arm away from Quinn's grasp. "What did you do that for? I was just going to say I was sorry, even though it wasn't really my fault."

"That was them," Quinn said.

"Who?" Cody asked.

"The two people we saw snooping around Skeleton Man's house!"

Chapter 9

When the radio alarm clicked on at 0530 military time—5:30 a.m.—Cody jolted awake. Pulling off her puffy comforter that had completely covered her head, she gasped for air. Seconds earlier, she'd had the distinct sensation of being smothered by a large woman in a flowery dress.

Lying back down, Cody glanced at the radio alarm. She slapped the Snooze button, shutting off Acne's latest hit, "Everything Stinks." Five thirty? It felt like the middle of the night. In fact, it was about the same time Skeleton Man's house had caught on fire the previous morning.

She glanced at her ceiling. The glow-in-the-dark stick-on stars shone brightly. It was way too early for school. In fact, it was too early for anything.

Just before she drifted off again, her eyes sprang open again. She'd almost forgotten! The alarm hadn't been set for school. It was for the clandestine meeting of the Code Busters. They were supposed to meet in front of Skeleton Man's charred house at 0600 sharp.

She had less than thirty minutes to get ready.

Moving into hyper-speed, Cody ran through her usual morning rituals. By five minutes to six, she was dressed in a fresh pair of jeans, yellow tank top, flip-flops, and red hoodie, with her hair in a ponytail. Although there was a chill in the early morning air, the day would turn warm by noon—perfect for her cool-weather fashion statement.

Holding a cinnamon bagel in one hand and her backpack in the other, Cody slipped out the door, closing it quietly. She'd left a note on the kitchen table to let her mother know she'd be meeting M.E. early so they could go over their spelling words before the test. It was partly true.

The street was eerily deserted as Cody crossed over to Skeleton Man's house; the area was lit only by the nearby streetlight. Moments later Quinn appeared, wearing a RELATIVITY IS ALL RELATIVE T-shirt and khaki slacks, followed by Luke, who wore his usual skater shorts, oversize shirt, and Vans. M.E. arrived minutes later, in red tights, a tie-dyed skirt, and Ed Hardy tattoo-style T-shirt.

"Yo," Luke said, yawning. M.E. groaned loudly.

"*Quiet!*" Quinn hissed. He glanced up and down the street. "We don't want to get caught before we even start."

Cody turned to the gutted house. Even in the

dawning morning light the place looked creepy. Outside, the wood was scorched black. Quinn walked into the backyard and waved the others to follow him. Once inside the yard, they ducked behind the fence.

"We'll go around the back where no one can see us," Quinn whispered.

As she passed by the front of the house, Cody caught sight of the yellow caution tape and a sign that read, NO TRESPASSING! KEEP OUT! DANGER! Uh-oh. They were probably doing something illegal. If her mother found out…

"No one will see us here," Quinn said, as the group collected at the back door of the house. The yard was filled with metal sculptures that blocked the view of most neighbors.

"I'm not so sure this is a good idea," M.E. said, gawking at the soot that had collected on her shoes. Cody noticed her own toes were black. Wearing flip-flops had not been the best idea.

"We'll just take a quick look around and see if there's anything like a safe or a will or gold," Quinn said. "Then we're outta here, okay?"

The others nodded. Quinn tried the doorknob. It came off in his hand. Luke stepped up, grasped the hole where the knob had once been, and yanked the door open. After brushing the soot off his hands, he stepped inside. Quinn, Cody, and M.E. followed him into the shell of the old man's home.

Cody wrinkled her nose at the lingering smell of charred wood. She scanned the interior, her eyes wide with a mixture of horror and wonder. The interior walls appeared rippled and shiny, like a frozen waterfall. Everything was shiny black or shades of gray. Some of the furniture had melted, while other pieces were just charred remains, like bony skeletons. She stepped carefully to avoid broken glass, while trying to identify blackened objects that looked surreal.

"Let's split up," Quinn said, checking his military

watch. "We'll make better time. M.E., you check the bathroom; Luke, the living room; and Cody, the kitchen. I'll search the back room."

Cody tiptoed into the kitchen, hoping the floor didn't cave in. She marveled at the spectacle in shimmering black. Although the walls, floor, and ceiling remained, they were scorched and ripply. The appliances had melted and blistered and were covered with a shiny black skin. The room looked as if all the color had been sucked out.

After a few minutes of searching the gutted cupboards, Cody found one cupboard door intact. She pulled it open and spotted a bunch of medicine bottles, unharmed by the fire. *Wow*, Cody thought as she glanced at the unfamiliar labels. *Skeleton Man must have been sick.* She tried to pronounce the various medications: Citi-something, Tenecte-something, Cere-something.

I wonder what was wrong with him, she thought.

After making certain there was nothing left to explore in the kitchen, Cody returned to the front hallway and met up with the others. Quinn had a black smudge on his cheek and black fingertips. Luke had handprints on his shorts from wiping his sooty hands. M.E.'s black-and-white athletic shoes were now just black. Cody would have to scrub her feet *and* her face and hands before going to school. "Find anything?" Quinn asked, wiping his forehead and leaving a black streak.

Cody shook her head.

"Nothing," Luke said.

"Me, neither," added M.E. "I think we better go." She glanced around nervously. "This whole place could fall down on us any minute. I saw it in a movie once." She started for the back door.

"Wait!" Quinn grabbed her arm with a filthy hand.

"No, Quinn," Cody said. "M.E.'s right. It's too dangerous in here. And there's no sign of anything like money or treasure. We checked everywhere but upstairs, and we can't get up there because the staircase is too damaged for—"

Cody stopped. Catching a movement in the corner of her eye, she turned to see Luke waving at them from the hallway.

"Hey, look at this." Luke was pointing at something on the wall.

It appeared to be a framed certificate, scorched but not completely charred, hanging by a thin wire. Although the glass had shattered from the intense heat, the frame was intact and dangled crookedly on the wall. The certificate inside was severely singed, with only a few readable letters remaining in one undamaged corner.

Quinn read the letters aloud.

"Looks like...C I A..."

"Dude," Luke said, blinking rapidly. "You think Skeleton Man was a *spy* for the Central Intelligence Agency?"

Quinn peered at the letters. "Maybe. He was always staring out his window and watching us."

Cody pointed to an imprint on the certificate. "There's some kind of official emblem."

Quinn reached out to touch the raised design, but as soon as his fingers made contact, the paper crumbled into bits and drifted to the ground like black snow.

"Dang," Quinn said, frowning.

Cody glanced back at the frame. "Hey…there's something hidden behind the paper. It looks like…a piece of metal."

She reached up and tried to pull the frame from the wall, but it fell apart in her hands, the pieces dropping to the floor. Bending over, she retrieved the metal object, which had come loose. It was about the size of an Altoids container. She blew off the black dust, then ran her fingers over the smooth top. She flipped it over and noticed the underside felt rougher than the top. Holding it up in the dim light, she tried to catch a reflection. That's when she noticed the smudges she'd left on the bottom of the tin.

She caught her breath.

"There's something written on this!" Her dirty hand had left particles of ash inside the indentations. Quickly, she swiped her other hand over the surface, cleaning off the residue, while at the same time depositing ash in the tiny crevices.

The darkened words jumped out at her.

WILL you find **THE** money?

No, it's not **INSIDE**.

LIES are in the **ASH**es.

Not a place to hide.

Cody felt a wave of excitement. This was definitely a message of some kind. From Skeleton Man?

"Okay, that's just weird," M.E. said aloud.

Quinn's eyes grew wide. "I *told* you there was

something valuable hidden in this house. This *proves* it!"

M.E. frowned. "Quinn, this doesn't prove anything. It doesn't even make sense. If it's supposed to be a poem, it doesn't rhyme. And even if we could figure out what it means, it doesn't prove that there's money or a will hidden around here."

"I think Quinn's right," Cody said. "It's some kind of code or puzzle."

"And we have to solve it," Quinn added. "I mean, if Skeleton Man worked for the CIA, he probably used a lot of codes. He's not going to just *tell* people where to look for his treasure."

"It doesn't look like any puzzle we've ever solved before," Luke said, leaning over Cody's shoulder to see the object better. "And if he really worked for the CIA, this isn't going to be an easy code to crack."

Cody, who'd been studying the puzzle while the others argued, drew in her breath.

"What's wrong, Cody?" M.E. asked. "You look

like you've seen a ghost."

Cody pointed to the second-to-last line of the puzzle and read it aloud. "Listen. It says, 'Lies are in the ashes.'"

"Yeah, so?" M.E. asked, scrunching up her face.

"If Skeleton Man wrote this, don't you think it's a little weird that he'd use the word *ashes*?" Cody looked at their blank faces. She picked up a handful of the feathery silt from the floor and let it sift between her fingers. "How did Skeleton Man know his house was going to burn down?"

"Unless he planned it, and set fire to it himself...," M.E. said.

Before they had time to think about it further, Cody heard a noise coming from the living room. She grabbed M.E.'s arm and pointed to the source of the sound.

"I heard something," she mouthed, barely breathing. "It came from behind the couch!"

Chapter 10

Just as Cody was about to make a dash for the door, a streak of black lightning shot past her from behind the couch.

"Eeeek!" M.E. screamed, ducking behind Luke. "What was that?"

The black ghost seemed to have vanished into thin air.

Quinn blew out a deep breath of air. "It was just

one of Skeleton Man's cats. The SPCA was here last night, picking them up. I guess they missed that one."

M.E. came out from behind Luke and looked in the direction of the black cat's path. "Poor thing! Here, kitty, kitty," she called. "Where did it go?"

Cody pointed toward a broken window. "I thought I saw it run through there, but I'm not sure. It was moving pretty fast." Cody took a step toward the window, then stopped abruptly.

"Shhhh!" she hushed the others. "Someone's coming! Quick! Hide! Back in there!" She pointed to the living room.

"Hope it's not the cops," Luke whispered as he darted into the living room. The others followed, and all four ducked behind the charred couch where the cat had been hiding only moments ago.

Seconds later they heard a key in the front door lock.

Then footsteps in the hall.

Cody and the others crouched down, not breathing, ears alert. If it were the police, the kids would surely be discovered, Cody thought. And then what would happen to them? Would they be hauled off to juvenile hall for breaking and entering or illegal trespass or whatever they called it on *CSI*? Her cop mother and lawyer dad would just love that. She'd be grounded until college.

The footsteps grew louder as the intruders entered the living room. Cody tried not to breathe, but her lungs were tightening. She hoped the cramps in her legs would ease before she collapsed and gave away their hiding place.

Something small and warm touched the side of Cody's leg. She startled.

A rat?

Or worse?

What could be worse than a rat?

Whatever it was had come from under the couch.

She shivered, suddenly feeling chilled. What if the rumors were true? What if the house really was...haunted? She bit into her lip to hold back a scream from escaping.

She felt the movement again. There was something definitely touching her leg.

Something alive.

And furry.

She bent down, straining to see under the couch in the semidarkness, hoping her joints wouldn't crack. A black paw reached out and stroked her leg.

The black ghost cat! It had returned to the couch.

Cody reached underneath and swept the animal into her arms. To keep it quiet, she began petting it, then realized the cat's black color was coming off in her hands.

This was no black cat! It was Punkin! Covered in soot.

She kept a tight hold on him, stroking him behind

the ears to keep him from darting out and attracting the attention of the intruders.

The cat began to purr.

Loudly.

The footsteps in the living room came to an abrupt halt.

Silence.

Then, a man's squeaky voice: "What was that?"

"I don't know," came a woman's booming voice. "Sounded like it came from over there."

Cody couldn't see where the woman pointed, but she felt dots of sweat break out on her forehead. She tightened her grip on Punkin.

Bad move. The cat arched its back, gave a loud caterwaul, and leaped from Cody's arms into the open.

Someone screamed.

Cody froze. They were sure to be discovered now.

Expecting footsteps to head her way any second,

Cody signaled to the others in sign language to be ready to run. She figured it was their only hope. She began counting down, holding up one finger, then two...Just as she was about to raise the third finger, one of the intruders spoke again.

"Jeepers, Jezebel! Do you have to scream like that?" the male voice croaked. "You nearly busted my eardrums...and I'm already half deaf from all your yapping. It was just one of Junior's stupid cats."

"Well, it nearly scared the pee out of me, Jasper!" the woman named Jezebel cried. "I almost wet my pants."

Cody slowly peeked out from behind the couch to get a quick look at the two people in the growing light. As she suspected, it was the couple she and Quinn had spotted on Skeleton Man's porch the other night.

The man called Jasper was shorter and thinner than the woman. He wore a rumpled, mismatched suit that looked like it came from the thrift shop, and scuffed dad-type shoes. His sparse comb-over hair looked pasted to his mostly bald head.

Jezebel was twice his size, with big frizzy hair, a big flowery dress, sagging knee-highs, and heel-less slippers. She'd overdone the makeup and looked like a clown with too much red lipstick, pink blush, and purple eye shadow.

Cody ducked back down out of sight.

"It's *them*!" she mouthed to the others.

"You're always peeing your pants, Jez," the man mumbled. "If you'd quit screaming all the time, maybe that wouldn't happen so much."

"Shut up, Jasper, you old fart. I wet my pants 'cause that's what old ladies do. At least I don't stink up the place like you." Cody heard her sniff the air. "What's that rancid smell, anyway? Your breakfast?"

Jasper let a loud one rip.

Cody nearly wet her own pants trying to stifle

a laugh. Luke held his nose, while Quinn covered his mouth to keep himself from laughing out loud. M.E. buried her face in her hands.

"That's the smell of money, Jezebel," Jasper said, laugh-snorting. "Junior's money. And we better get to finding it before the cops come and clear us outta here. This place is probably condemned, you know. It could come falling down on us any second."

Cody heard something land on the floor behind her and jumped. A seared picture had fallen down from its spot on the scorched wall. She hoped the two intruders didn't decide to investigate it.

"What was that?" Jasper asked.

Jezebel sighed. "Oh, don't be such a scaredy-cat, Jasper. It was just a falling picture frame. Now quit farting around. Remember, if we don't find that money, we won't be able to help your dear ailing cousin with his health care and widdle puddy tats."

Hmmm, Cody thought. They might be weird, but maybe they really cared about Skeleton Man, and that's why they were looking for the money. Maybe she and the Code Busters Club members could help them find it.

Cody was about to step out from her hiding place to offer assistance when she heard a pair of hideous cackles.

They were laughing!

She'd almost believed those two were here to help.

"Of course, if something should happen to my dear cousin, I guess we'd have to use some of the money for his funeral," Jasper said, still giggling.

"Yeah, twenty bucks ought to buy him a nice pine box, don't you think?" asked Jezebel. "Maybe we could bury him right out there in his own yard with all his ugly sculptures. We'd save a bundle that way."

"And we could use the rest of the dough for our own health care, just like you said, Jez," Jasper continued. "There's nothing like a cruise to Mexico, a new Cadillac, and a condo in Maui to improve your health!"

Cody couldn't believe her ears. These so-called relatives were just wolves in tacky clothing!

More snorts and cackles accompanied footsteps as Jasper and Jezebel shuffled out of the living room and into another part of the house.

Cody turned to the others and finger-spelled a word: .

Code Buster's Key and Solution found on pp. 202, 206.

The four club kids waited, not moving, behind the couch, as they listened to the footsteps returning to the hallway. Cody wondered what the "cousins" were doing.

"Find anything?" Jezebel growled. Cody heard the woman brush off her hands.

"Nothing!" Jasper snapped.

"Well, it's gotta be here somewhere," Jezebel said. "I'll bet that old ape-faced cousin of yours hid it and then made a puzzle out of it. He was always doing things like that—making up mysteries and such, before he got woo-woo in the head. He probably knew we'd come after it when he was gone."

"Yeah," Jasper said. "And if he wasn't right in the head when he hid it, we might never figure it out."

"Well, we ain't going to find anything standing around here," Jezebel said. "We gotta tear this place apart. But we'll need a few tools from the hardware store first, like a saw and a hammer. Come on. Let's get out of here before the cops find us. I don't want to answer a bunch of stupid questions. We'll come back later when we've got our supplies."

Cody and the others listened as the couple headed out the door. They waited a few minutes until the coast was clear, then Quinn peeked out over the top of the couch.

"They're gone," he whispered. His gelled, spiked hair had gone flat from all the nervous head rubbing he'd done.

Luke stood up and checked his watch. "Great! We're going to be late! We'll have to run all the way to school or we'll get detention. My *grandmère* will have my hide."

"What about Punkin?" Cody asked, glancing around. The ghost cat seemed to have disappeared again. "We can't just leave him here alone. He'll starve to death."

"He'll be okay until this afternoon," Quinn said. "We can come back after school and look for him if he doesn't turn up."

"Dude, what about the money or the will or whatever?" Luke said. "We've got to find it before those two creeps come back and steal it."

"Wouldn't it be great if we actually found some kind of treasure?" Cody asked. "We could use it to help Skeleton Man's—I mean, Mr. Skelton's—cats."

Her mother didn't like it when she used the nick-name for the old, eccentric man. And now that he was in the hospital, Cody didn't feel good about it, either.

M.E. tapped her temple. "Sure sounds as if he was mental. Maybe that's why he was a hermit."

"We can't let those two get the money just to go on a cruise, that's for sure," Quinn added. "Now let's get out of here. We'll make a plan after school."

Cody led the way out the back door, bending down as she hurried around the side of the house. She prayed the neighbors wouldn't spot them. If she was late for school again this year, she'd get a Saturday detention. Saturdays were holy days to Cody—her one day to be with her father, who took her to a movie or the university museum or the Oakland Zoo. She couldn't let detention interfere with that.

"Hurry," she said, glancing back at the others as

she turned the corner. "We've only got five—"

"Watch out!" Quinn yelled.

Too late.

As Cody rounded the corner, she ran smack into what looked like a flower-covered refrigerator. The blow knocked her and the giant bouquet to the ground.

For a few seconds, Cody couldn't breathe. She'd had the air knocked out of her before, and it was a scary feeling—as if she'd never be able to breathe again. But seconds later she caught her breath. She stood up and brushed herself off. A smear of red covered her left arm.

Blood?

She swiped it with a finger. Lipstick.

"Jeez Louise, would you watch it!" The giant bunch of flowers known as Jezebel wheezed as she tried to catch her own breath. She lay flat on her back on the ground, her floral print dress up around her waist, displaying giant granny underpants with little hearts on them.

Luke groaned at the sight and turned away. "Duuude!"

"I'm...s-so sorry!" Cody stammered. She reached down and offered a hand to the woman.

Jezebel swatted Cody's hand away. "You kids get on out of here!" she screeched. She pushed herself onto her elbows, then sat up and attempted to pull down her skirt. "This here is private property. You kids have no business being here!"

Jasper, who'd been watching the scene from behind one of Skeleton Man's metal sculptures, stepped forward timidly. "Yeah. You kids are, uh, trespassing. I'm going to, uh, call the cops."

Jezebel rolled her eyes at him.

That's all Cody needed—her mother showing up to arrest her. "I...we..."

Quinn slipped on his aviator glasses and said, "We were just looking for her cat. We saw him run into this yard. Blackish orange? Long tail? Yellow eyes? Maybe you saw him?" He pretended to look around the front yard.

"No, I ain't seen no cat." Jezebel rolled over onto her knees and stuck her behind in the air in an attempt to stand up. The kids almost laughed out loud. "Jasper! Help me up, you old fool!"

Jasper grabbed her fleshy arms and tried to pull her up, but she was too much for him. She finally shoved him away and pushed herself to standing, using a nearby sculpture for support. Jasper brushed off the leaves and weeds that clung to her dress, but he couldn't reach the ones stuck in her big bouffant helmet hair. The red lipstick smudge on her cheeks and chin matched the streak on Cody's arm, and gave Jezebel a hideous, deformed-looking mouth.

The four club members began backing up to the front gate. "Sorry to bother you, ma'am," M.E. called. "We're leaving now. No need for the police."

She made a dash for the opened gate, followed by the others. They broke into a run toward school and away from the angry glares coming from Jezebel and Jasper.

Cody glanced back just before she turned the corner at the end of the street and caught a last glimpse of the couple. They were still standing in the yard, their arms crossed over their chests, their eyes intent on the kids.

Cody looked down at her outfit. She wondered if they had noticed that her clothes were covered in soot. If they had, they'd know the truth: that the kids had been inside the house.

Snooping.

Chapter 11

With two minutes to spare before the first bell, Cody and M.E. stopped by the girls' bathroom to clean off the soot. After the fifteenth paper towel, Cody knew it was a wasted effort. All they'd managed to do was smear the black spots into gray streaks. Lucky for M.E., she was wearing red tights. The gray stripes just made them look cool, like an abstract painting. Unfortunately, the stripes on the back of Cody's shorts made her butt look like a mutant zebra's.

"Hee-haw!" Matt the Brat snorted at Cody. "Awesome stripes. Is there a zebra missing from the zoo? Or did you escape from Alcatraz?" He laughed, sending drops of flying spit everywhere.

Cody glared at the school bully as she passed him on the way to her seat. Today his green-sprayed buzz cut looked like a lawn in desperate need of a mowing. The color matched the fake tattoo of a two-headed snake on his puffy arm. His oversize skull-and-crossbones T-shirt barely reached the waistband of his sagging, baggy jeans, and every now and then Cody caught an unwelcome glimpse of his tighty whiteys. It was enough to make her lose her breakfast.

Even though Matt the Brat acted like a jerk and smelled like peanut butter and called everyone names, he didn't really scare Cody. She'd seen him cry once, after he'd come out of the principal's office.

In fact, he'd been in trouble so many times, he had his own special chair there. Cody knew if Matt the Brat even burped too loud these days, he was apt to be expelled from Berkeley Co-op Middle School.

As soon as she sat down in her assigned seat behind Matt, Cody checked her backpack. She unzipped the largest compartment and felt around inside, bypassing her school notebook, codebook, pencil, and other supplies.

She shuddered.

The case the kids had found at Skeleton Man's house was gone.

Quickly, she unzipped another compartment and jammed her hand inside. Nothing except some ABC gum and a few cat-shaped erasers. She tried another compartment, then another. In the last compartment, the smallest one that she rarely used, she felt the cold hard metal against her fingertips.

She breathed a sigh of relief. *The case! Thank goodness.*

If she lost Skeleton Man's metal box—the one they'd discovered hidden behind the certificate—she'd never hear the end of it from the Code Busters. Luckily, she'd had the presence of mind to stuff it into her backpack when Jezebel and Jasper had arrived—even if she'd forgotten exactly where.

She pulled the case from its hiding place and turned it over in her hands. Ms. Stadelhofer was busy calling roll, so Cody didn't have to pay close attention until her teacher got to the Js. She checked the case more closely. While the box resembled a mint container, it appeared to be handmade. The metal—dark and rusty—reminded her of the kind of metal Skeleton Man used for his yard sculptures. Turning it over again, Cody searched for a way to open it.

"Dakota Jones?" Stad called.

Cody was so deep in thought while trying to open the box, she was startled to hear her name. Matt the Brat turned around in his chair, grinning wetly.

"Uh, here," she said, raising her hand.

Before she could lower her hand, Matt made a swipe at the case, knocking it to the floor with a loud *clink!*

The whole class turned toward Cody. She blushed as she leaned over to retrieve the case.

"Dakota?"

Cody looked up at the face of Ms. Stadelhofer looming over her, frowning.

"I...dropped my...," she started to say.

Stad held out a freckled hand. "I'll take that. You may have it back at lunch. Until then, it remains on my desk with the other confiscated objects. You know the rules."

Cody slowly placed the case in Ms. Stadelhofer's outstretched hand. Matt the Brat snorted, and Cody knew he was enjoying her humiliation immensely. Matt's philosophy was: If Matt the Brat couldn't have it, nobody could. No matter *what* it was.

As Stad walked back to her desk, Matt

whispered, "What's so special about that stupid box anyway? Do you keep your little treasures in there? Or is that your makeup case—"

"Matthew Jeffreys," Ms. Stadelhofer called from her desk. "Turn around. Eyes front. Pencil in hand."

Cody gave Matt a wicked smile as he turned to face the teacher. She'd have to keep an eye on the Brat until she got that case back.

Worried about the metal case, Cody could hardly keep her mind on her social studies the rest of the morning. Luckily, Matt the Brat seemed to have forgotten all about it. He was busy bugging other kids and hadn't paid much attention to her after the incident.

All during a long and boring "trip" to some ancient civilization, Cody kept shifting her attention from the other confiscated items on Ms. Stad's desk— a silver iPod, a charm bracelet, a headset, some gummy worms, and a coded note that Samantha the Snoop had intercepted between Cody and M.E.—to the classroom clock hanging on the wall by the door.

On the dot of 11:59 a.m., she checked to make sure the metal case was still on Ms. Stad's desk. Quickly, she lifted the top of her desk, retrieved her books and papers, unzipped her backpack, stuffed everything inside, closed the desktop, and sat up straight to wait for the lunch bell. She stared intently at the clock, willing the long hand to click over to 12:00 noon.

The bell rang. Along with everyone else in class, Cody stood up and hoisted on her backpack. She ran for the teacher's desk, through the crowd of kids all trying to exit at the same time.

When she reached Ms. Stad's desk, she blinked in disbelief.

The case was missing.

And so was Matt the Brat.

• • •

"It's gone!" Cody said, grabbing M.E. on her way out of her classroom.

"What's gone?" M.E. frowned at Cody's worried face.

"The case! Ms. Stadelhofer took it and put it on her desk with the other stuff, but when I went to get it, it was gone!"

"Oh no," M.E. said. She waved over Quinn and Luke, who were headed for the cafeteria.

"'Sup?" Luke asked, as he and Quinn joined the two girls.

"The *case*. It's gone!" Cody squealed.

"Skeleton Man's case?" Quinn asked, lifting his sunglasses to eye Cody. He didn't look happy.

"Duuude," Luke said, which could have meant "No way" or "Not good" or any number of things.

"I *know*," Cody said, near tears. "I think Matt the Brat stole it!"

M.E. scanned the school grounds, then turned back to the group. "We've got to get it back. Let's spread out and see if we can find Matt. Cody, you try the cafeteria. Luke, check out the playing field. Quinn, he might be in the boy's bathroom, so look there. I'll see if he's hiding in back of the school."

The other three nodded and took off for their assigned areas. Cody headed for the cafeteria.

The noise level inside the large cafeteria was deafening, but Cody hardly noticed, intent on searching for Matt the Brat and getting back the case. After scanning the room twice, she finally spotted Matt sitting at a table with a tray full of food. His plate was untouched, definitely not normal for him. Cody immediately saw why. He was fiddling with something small in his hand.

Skeleton Man's case.

Cody moved in closer to make sure, being careful to keep herself hidden behind some other kids in case Matt looked up. At the moment, he was too busy trying to pry the metal box open with a fork to notice her. Luckily, it was a plastic fork. One of the tines broke off and flew across the table, landing in Samantha the Snoop's apple crisp opposite him.

"You dork!" Samantha said.

She shoved the dessert over to Matt to show him what he'd done. He ignored her and continued trying to open the case with the broken fork.

"What are you doing?" Samantha asked. "You can't open that with a plastic fork, dork. Try this." She pulled something out of her backpack.

A knife? Cody wondered. Boy, was she going to be in trouble.

Cody inched closer. She was only two tables away.

It wasn't a knife. It was a protractor from math class. Matt the Brat snatched the math tool from Samantha and began digging at the side of the case with the sharp end.

Great! Cody thought. *He's going to break it open*

with that thing! Frantically, she looked around for some way to stop him. She knew she couldn't do it alone.

That's when the idea hit her.

Cody ran out of the cafeteria, nearly knocking over a kid carrying a tray full of meat loaf and potatoes, and sped around the corner toward the school office.

She peered in and found the room empty. The secretary must have been on a bathroom break. *Yes!*

She ducked into the supply room, where the public address system was kept. Every morning the principal made announcements on the PA system—upcoming events, changes in the daily schedule, honorable mentions—along with a couple of lame jokes. Otherwise, it was used only in case of emergency.

That would be now, Cody thought.

Cody closed the door and sat down in the chair

opposite the microphone. She'd have to work fast before the secretary heard the sounds over the loudspeaker and came back to see Cody making them—that would mean detention for sure. And then her mother would kill her.

But she had to get that case back.

Switching on the "All-Campus" button, she turned the volume to high and began tapping on the head of the mic.

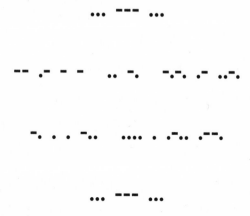

Code Buster's Key and Solution found on pp. 202, 207.

Chapter 12

When Cody was finished, she switched off the PA system and quickly slipped out of the office before the secretary returned and caught her. If the woman heard the tapping, Cody hoped she'd think there was some malfunction with the system and wouldn't recognize Morse code.

Moments later she met up with Luke, Quinn, and M.E. at the door to the cafeteria.

"Got your message," Luke said, scanning inside the room. "Where is he?"

Cody pointed out Matt the Brat, who, thankfully, was still working on the case with the sharp end of the protractor. They headed over, trying to keep a low profile so they wouldn't attract Matt's attention. As they got closer, Cody noticed Matt wasn't poking at the case anymore.

He was stabbing it.

Repeatedly.

It was sure to break open at any second.

"What do we do?" Cody whispered.

Luke looked down at a tray of leftover food on one of the nearby tables. He picked up a hard roll and threw it at Matt's hand. Being the athlete he was, it was a direct hit. The protractor flew out of Matt's grasp and landed on the pizza at the next table.

"Ow!" Matt screeched, shaking his hand and dropping the metal case. The case fell under the table. Right next to his giant smelly shoe.

Matt spun around and spotted Luke with a second roll in his hand. His face reddened with anger as he muttered, "Stupid code kids..."

Before Matt could bend down and retrieve the case, the pizza—minus the protractor—came flying at him from behind like a Frisbee. It bounced off the back of his head, leaving bits of salami, cheese, and tomato sauce glistening in his green buzz-cut hair. Matt grimaced as he reached behind him and pulled the pizza toppings off his head.

He stared at the mess in his hand for a second, his eyes wild, his face a blotchy red. Reaching for a chocolate-frosted brownie from a nearby tray, he grabbed it and shot-putted it in the direction of the pizza thrower.

Unfortunately for Matt, the brownie was intercepted by Ms. Stadelhofer, who had just stepped over to stop the budding food fight.

She took the brownie right in the face.

The Code Busters ducked under a table. Before Ms. Stadelhofer could blow her whistle, food started flying everywhere. Pizza, meat loaf, biscuits, brownies, and at least two kinds of vegetables went airborne, landing with splats around the chaotic lunchroom. Stad, wearing the remains of chocolate frosting on her nose, suddenly "got milk" when an open carton of low-fat milk hit her in the chest and drenched the front of her lavender silk blouse. When she managed to blow her whistle, the sound was ear piercing.

The Code Busters certainly know how to create a distraction, Cody thought, watching the food fly from under the table. Searching the area, she spotted the metal case about three feet away, under the next table. Crawling over, her knees collected bits of lime-green Jell-O with pineapple bits. She reached for the case.

A big shoe intercepted and kicked the case out of range.

Cody took a moment to wipe the green slime on someone's pant leg, then again crawled toward the case. This time when she reached it, she pounced on top of it. With it safely beneath her, she slithered backward under another table and then sat up. Before anything else could happen to the case, she stuffed it into her pants pocket.

Cody waved at Quinn, still under the first table, to get his attention. He removed his sunglasses, and she gave him a thumbs-up. He passed the signal behind him to M.E. and Luke, then gestured, military style, for the others to follow him, as he zigzagged on hands and knees beneath the connecting cafeteria tables until they all reached the exit.

They were about to spring to their feet when Principal Grunt appeared in the doorway. His face wasn't wearing its usual "school pride" expression. Instead, he held a megaphone in one hand and a whistle in the other.

Cody winced at the shrill sound as Principal

Grunt blew the whistle with a mighty breath.

"Matthew Jeffreys!" Grunt's voice boomed through the megaphone. Students decorated in a rainbow of cafeteria foods stopped midthrow and turned to the principal. They stood frozen, open-mouthed and wide-eyed.

All eyes followed the principal as he marched straight for Matt the Brat, who was holding a handful of soggy french fries in his raised hand.

The Code Busters took advantage of the distraction and ducked quietly out of the cafeteria doors. Standing in the doorway, Cody glanced back at Matt, his face glistening with sweat and some kind of sauce.

Principal Grunt stood facing Matt, arms crossed, his head shaking in disgust at the student he assumed had started the food fight. But Matt wasn't looking at the principal. He was staring straight at Cody, his sauce-covered face twisted in anger. Even at a distance, she had no trouble reading his lips as he mouthed the words: "You're *so* dead."

Cody didn't see Matt the Brat the rest of the day, thank goodness. She hoped he was in detention for the rest of the semester. When Ms. Stad appeared in class after lunch in a fresh blouse, her nose was shiny from washing off the brownie and milk. She spent the rest of the class time talking about the dangers of food fights and had the students break into "tribes" to "problem solve" future situations.

Cody could barely keep her mind on the topic, wondering what was inside the metal case that had caused so much trouble. She'd handed it over to Quinn as soon as they were away from the cafeteria, and Quinn had tucked it safely in his zippered jacket pocket. Her only worry now was Matt the Brat's threat: "You're *so* dead."

Detention wouldn't last forever.

When the last bell rang, Cody had to fight with

her desk to get a book out. When she got out to the hall, M.E. had disappeared. Cody headed for the flagpole, the Code Busters' usual meeting place, but there was no sign of any of her friends. Uh-oh. It looked like she'd have to walk to the clubhouse by herself.

Alone.

With Matt the Brat's threat hanging over her.

Not to mention the mountain lion.

Cody kept glancing behind her to check for Matt as she made her way down the street. Once she headed up the hill toward the clubhouse, she kept her eyes peeled for the lion. There was no sign of either one, although she jumped twice—once when a dog barked, and a second time when something behind one of the eucalyptus trees rustled. Running the rest of the way up the hill, she didn't know which was worse—a hungry mountain lion or an angry bully.

When she finally reached the clubhouse, she

gave the secret knock and password. The bolt was removed and the door opened, and Cody sighed with relief at finding Quinn and Luke there. But when she realized M.E. was not among them, she recalled Matt the Brat's words before he was hauled off to detention. Matt knew that even though Luke had started the food fight—*Matt* had gotten blamed. Cody's relief quickly turned to concern for her friend.

"Where's M.E.?" Cody glanced down the forested hill before closing the door and removing her backpack. She sat cross-legged on her hoodie to protect her legs from the cold sheet metal that made up the floor and hid their secret stash.

Quinn shrugged. "I haven't seen her since lunch. She usually comes with you."

Cody frowned. "I hope nothing's happened to her...."

Luke shook his head. "I know she's not the bravest person on the planet, but M.E. can take care of herself. She's quick and small, and she can talk her way out of anything. She's probably just—"

A familiar knock at the door interrupted Luke.

"That's probably her now," Luke said, rising to his feet. But before he opened the door, he asked, "What's the password?"

"*Yadsruht*," came a muffled voice.

Luke unbolted the door and opened it. It was M.E., all right.

But she wasn't alone.

"Dude! Who's your friend?" Luke gawked at the newcomer.

Cody leaped to her feet. "You found Punkin!" She took the orange cat from M.E.'s arms and stroked him. "Where was he?"

"I found him hiding behind one of those metal sculptures in Skeleton's yard," M.E. said. "He was meowing and clawing at the dirt."

"You went *back* there?" Cody asked, surprised at M.E. Normally, she was the first to chicken out when there was any kind of danger involved.

"I knew you missed him, Cody," M.E. said. "I wanted to surprise you."

"That's so sweet! You even cleaned the soot off him," Cody said, nearly tearing up as she rubbed the cat's soft fur.

"Hey," Luke said. "Let's make him the Code Buster's mascot. We could name him Decipher."

"I think we should name him Lucky," Quinn said. "He's lucky to be around."

"How about Bond—Cat Bond?" M.E. added in a funny British accent. "He'd make a great spy cat. Double-o-nine…lives." She giggled.

Cody shook her head. "Sorry, he already has a name—Punkin." She reached under the cat's neck to show them the personalized collar she'd made for him. But when she searched his fur, the tag felt different. She pulled it out and examined it.

"That's weird. The tag I made for him is covered with a sticker. And there's a small key attached."

She showed the tag and key to the others. "It's handwritten. It says, 'Francis Scott.' Is that the cat's name?"

"Francis Scott?" Luke and Quinn said at the same time.

"What kind of a name is that for a cat?" Quinn grimaced.

"It sounds familiar," Luke added.

"You're thinking of Francis Scott Key," Cody said. "He wrote the 'Star-Spangled Banner,' remember?"

"Hey, that's cool," Luke said. "There's a key, and his name is Francis Scott. Get it?"

"That reminds me…" Quinn pulled the metal case from his zippered jacket. "Look at this."

Luke squinted at the case. "What?"

"There are letters written on the side," Quinn answered. "You can see them when they catch the light."

"What do they say?" Cody asked, surprised that

she had missed them when she'd had the case.

"They're really faint," Quinn said, "but the soot from the fire makes them easier to read."

"Let me see." Cody took the case from Quinn's hands and looked at it closely. The writing was fancy and old-fashioned, like something she'd seen in books at museums. She could just make out three letters.

"F S K," Cody said.

"That's not a word," M.E. said.

"What's it supposed to mean?" Luke asked, raising an eyebrow.

"Good question," Quinn said, taking the case back from Cody.

"Maybe they're initials," M.E. suggested.

Quinn shook his head. "But the old man's name is Skeleton—I mean *Skelton*. That's his last name, not his middle name. Maybe the initials stand for something in code, like in that framed CIA certificate we saw. FSK. Federal…Secret…Ka…"

He shrugged and placed the case into Luke's outstretched hand.

Luke studied it intently, then said, "Dude, I got nothing. If we don't have the key, we can't break the code."

Cody sat up. "That's it!"

"What's it?" Luke asked.

"What you said about the key, Luke," Cody continued. "Mr. Skelton stuck that note on the tag, wrote that name, and attached a key. It must mean his name is—"

They all said it at once: "Francis Scott *Key*!"

Cody looked at the cat.

"The 'key' to the metal case is around the cat's neck!"

Chapter 13

Punkin, aka Francis Scott Key, seemed to understand every word the kids said. Apparently, he didn't want any part of it. He arched his back, let out a howl, and darted from Cody's hands.

"Get him!" Quinn shouted. "Otherwise, he'll get out through the space under the door."

When the kids built the clubhouse, it hadn't been

perfectly square. There was just enough room for a big rat or small cat to squeeze through the gap under the door. More than once, the kids had discovered an animal waiting for them in the clubhouse—mostly squirrels and raccoons. But one time they had found a skunk that had smelled up the place so bad, they had had to use Quinn's backyard toolshed for meetings until the clubhouse had aired out.

Punkin instinctively seemed to know about the escape route and made a run for the space under the door. But Luke was too fast for him and blocked the opening by sticking his leg in front of the door. The cat hissed at Luke, but Luke didn't budge.

"Nice kitty," he said, as Cody picked up Punkin and tried to calm him.

"Uh-oh," Quinn said, searching the floor around them. "Where'd the case go?" The kids had lost track of it during the cat's escape attempt.

"There it is," M.E. said, spotting it under Cody's

backpack. Cody lifted up the case with her free hand, her other hand still holding Punkin close to her chest. She turned to M.E. and asked, "M.E., can you get the key off the cat?"

M.E. nodded, reached over, and felt around the collar for the buckle. In seconds the key dangled from her fingertips.

"Try the key in that little opening," Cody said, indicating the small slit on the side of the case. M.E. inserted the key and, with a twist of her wrist, popped open the metal case.

"Cool!" Luke said, and high-fived Cody.

Quinn grinned with anticipation as M.E. lifted the lid and looked inside.

Her wide eyes narrowed. "There's nothing in here. It's totally empty."

Cody took the opened case to see for herself. M.E. was right—there was nothing inside. She turned the box around and checked it more closely. As she started to close the lid, her eyes caught on something she hadn't noticed when she'd held the case upright. There were faint scratches on the inside of the lid.

Cody looked at her friend M.E. "M.E., do you have a candy bar?" Cody knew M.E. had a sweet tooth and almost always had something chocolate in her backpack.

"Maybe," M.E. said, grasping her backpack tightly. "Why?"

"Hand it over," Cody said, holding out her hand.

"No way."

"Please."

M.E. frowned and opened a small compartment in her backpack. "You owe me," she said, passing Cody a chocolate bar.

Cody handed over Punkin to M.E., then ripped open the wrapper and broke off a piece of the chocolate coating. She pressed it between her fingers until it melted, then smeared it over the scratches. Using her palm, she wiped away the excess. The melted chocolate had filled the small indentations of the etched metal, making them more visible.

"These look like tiny drawings," she said, moving the lid back and forth to catch the light. "They're the same kind of drawings we saw on Mr. Skelton's window, Quinn."

Code Buster's Key and Solution found on pp. 203, 207.

Quinn studied the inside of the lid. "Wait a minute...." He stood up and motioned for the others to do the same. Bending down on one knee, he lifted up part of the metal floor, revealing half of the secret hiding place underneath. He reached inside and pulled out a worn copy of *Dictionary of Secret Codes*, then replaced the flooring. Flipping through it, he found what he was looking for—a chapter that featured stick figures holding flags at various angles.

Cody peered over his shoulder. "What are those?"

"Semaphores," Quinn said. "Sailors use flags, holding them at different angles, to represent letters." He studied the first stick figure, then ran his finger down the various semaphores and their matching alphabet letters. He stopped at the figure next to the letter U.

"Cody, write this down," he ordered.

Cody pulled out her codebook and flipped to a blank page.

"U," he said, his finger moving on to the next semaphore. One by one, he said them aloud. "N. D. E. R. C. O. U. C. H."

Cody wrote each letter as Quinn said it. When he stopped and closed the book, she read the word: *UNDERCOUCH*. "Under couch!" she announced excitedly.

"So those stick figures we saw on the window—I'll bet they were semaphores, too," Quinn said. "He was trying to send us a message."

Cody quickly flipped through her notebook to the page where she'd copied the figures from Skeleton Man's window. Borrowing the code dictionary, she began writing down letters to match each of the four stick figures. When she was done, she closed the book and looked at her three friends.

"H. E. L. P.," she said. "He was trying to tell us he needed help!"

"We've got to go back there," Quinn said.

"Where?" M.E. said.

"Skeleton Man's house," Quinn said, stuffing the codebook into his backpack and pulling out his aviator glasses.

"Why?" Luke asked.

"Isn't it obvious? He left this coded message that says 'under couch.' He's obviously hidden something under his couch. We have to find it—before his two creepy cousins do."

"He's right," Luke said to the others. "We gotta check it out."

"But if the treasure is there, maybe the fire destroyed it," M.E. said.

Cody shook her head. "I don't think that's going to be a problem."

M.E. scrunched her nose. "Why not?"

"The couch frame was metal, like Skeleton Man's sculptures, so it didn't burn. He probably made it himself, like he made all those yard sculptures. If he's got something hidden, like a treasure, it's probably under the couch. Maybe in the floor."

Quinn jumped to his feet. "We better get over there. Now!"

Ducking behind Skeleton Man's fence, Cody, still holding the cat, and the others sneaked along the bushes, making their way to the back door of the burned-out house. She noticed immediately that something was different about the door. She yanked at it; it opened an inch, then jerked to a stop.

"Someone put a chain inside the door!" she said.

Luke tried to reach inside to unhook it but couldn't fit his hand through the opening. Neither could M.E., who had the smallest hands.

"Who would do that?" Quinn asked, obviously disturbed by this new roadblock.

"Maybe those two weirdos?" Luke guessed. His face brightened. "Wait a minute. I'll be right back." He took off running, disappearing around the side of the house. He returned a few seconds later, his face fallen. "The front door has a new knob—and it's locked, too."

"We're locked out," Luke said, then looked around. "We can't go through the windows. The ones that are broken have bars on them."

"I've got an idea," Cody said, spotting the cat door. The opening was about the size of a large shoebox, and was handmade from metal—another one of Mr. Skelton's creations.

She pushed the flap. It didn't move. Luke, getting the idea, sat down and gave it a kick, knocking it off one hinge. The door swung in, then dangled crookedly on the other hinge.

"Quinn, help me pull this thing off," Luke said, holding the flap in both hands. Quinn grabbed the other side of the small door and together they yanked at it. Quinn gave it an extra kick and the door came off in their hands, causing both of them to fall back on their bottoms.

"You did it!" M.E. squealed, scaring the cat in Cody's arms. Punkin leaped to the ground and ran through the opening, disappearing from sight.

"Sorry!" M.E. clapped a hand over her mouth.

"I guess you'll have to go in after him," Cody said, with a raised eyebrow and an evil grin.

M.E. looked up at her and shook her head. "There's no way I can crawl through that cat door. I'll never fit. No *way*, Jose."

"I'm kidding," Cody confessed. "But if you could fit your arm in there..."

"I can't reach the chain from down there. I've got the shortest arms!" M.E. said.

Cody turned her attention to Luke, the tallest in the group. "Luke, you've got to try to reach that chain and undo it."

"Me?" Luke asked, blinking. With a shrug, he lay down on the dirty porch, placing his head near the opening, and reached in.

"It's too far," Luke said, grunting as he struggled to reach the lock. "I need a stick or something."

Cody searched the yard for something that would help. The place was filled with metal sculptures; many of them looked like trees, and a few looked like cats. She found one with a three-foot branch that looked as if it were bent, and wiggled it back and forth. It broke in her hands. She brought it back to Luke.

He took the long metal stick and guided it in through the cat door opening. Aiming it upward, he began brushing it against the chain, trying to hook it. After several attempts, he latched onto the chain and slid it to the opening. Cody heard the chain fall open.

"We're in!" Quinn said, helping Luke to his feet and brushing off his back. "Nice work." Luke and Quinn bumped knuckles.

Cody and M.E. rolled their eyes.

The Code Busters slipped in through the door and headed for the couch. Quinn knelt down to look underneath and spotted Punkin. Gently, he pulled the cat from his hiding place and handed him to Cody. He knelt down again. "I think there's something *here*!" he whispered.

"What? The treasure?" Cody asked, tingling with excitement. The others got down on their knees to look underneath the metal frame.

"It's just a bunch of little holes," Luke said, shaking his head.

"Wait a minute," Cody said, running her fingers along the indentations. "This could be a message."

"What, like Morse code?" Quinn suggested.

"No, it's not Morse code. But it might be Braille," Cody said.

"I haven't learned Braille yet," Quinn said, frowning.

"I know the letters of my name in Braille." Cody sat back and dug out her notebook. She copied the pattern of holes onto a sheet of paper.

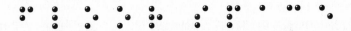

Code Buster's Key and Solution found on pp. 204, 207.

Then she wrote her name in Braille.

"Look. The third symbol could be an *O*. And it's repeated twice. That's an *S*, an *A*, and an *E*."

"So you've got *blank-OO-blank-S-blank-A-blank-E*," M.E. said, reading the letters Cody had jotted down underneath the corresponding dots. "We're missing a bunch of letters."

"I know my initials," Luke said. "That's an *L*." He pointed to the second set of dots.

Cody added it to the translated message. It now read: *blank-LOO-blank-S-blank-A-blank-E*.

"Still no clue," M.E. said, sounding discouraged.

"Oh wait! I also know my nickname in Braille—Cody." Cody added the letter *C* between the *A* and the *E*. "Loo sace," she said aloud, then repeated the sounds, adding letters to come up with familiar words—"ploom shace, blood slace, floor space...That's it!"

The kids looked at one another.

"Move the couch," Cody commanded. Luke and Quinn shoved the couch aside.

Quinn knelt down again and rolled up the charred throw rug. It smelled like burned rubber to Cody, and she crinkled her nose. Then, moving his hands over the bare floor, Quinn located a loose plank. He lifted it up.

The girls gasped.

The boys high-fived.

Cody whispered, "It looks like Skeleton Man's safe!"

Chapter 14

"Dude, open it!" Luke said, his eyes wide with anticipation.

Quinn looked at the safe's combination. Instead of numbers, he found alphabet letters from *A* to *Z*. He spun the lock around a few times, trying various words—*Skelton*, the name of the street, *Francis Scott Key*, even *Abracadabra* and *Open Sesame*.

Nothing worked.

"I don't suppose anyone knows the combination," Quinn said, giving up.

Cody grinned. "Actually, I think I might."

"Yeah, *right*," Quinn said.

Cody knelt down, handed Punkin to M.E., and turned the combination lock. The others watched as she worked. "First to the right…to 'F'…then to the left…'S'…then back to the right…"

"To the letter *K*!" M.E. said, petting the cat. "The cat's initials."

Cody stopped at the letter *K* and gave a tug.

The safe creaked open.

"Yes!" M.E. said.

Quinn frowned and asked, "How did you know?"

"Lucky guess?" Cody stifled a smile.

Luke elbowed her gently in the ribs. "No way, dude. How'd you do it?"

Cody couldn't keep the secret any longer. "Well, I just figured, since everything so far has been about Francis Scott, the cat had to be the *key* to the combination lock."

"Brilliant," M.E. said, grinning.

Cody reached into the safe, felt around, and pulled out a piece of paper. Her smile disappeared. "There's no money in here. Just this piece of paper."

"Oh great. *Another* code." Quinn sighed.

Cody unfolded the paper. After taking a deep breath, she read the handwritten note aloud. Again, some of the words were darker than others.

"**INSIDE LIES** a puzzle,

Where there should be cash.

WILL you find **THE** money?

Or be left with **ASH**?"

"Oookaaay," Luke said, scratching his head and readjusting his hat. "Now what?"

"Can I see the note?" Quinn asked. Cody handed it over. "That's weird...."

"What's weird?" M.E. asked.

"This note. It's a lot like the first one—that poem—we found inside the case, remember? Something about 'behind the frame.'"

"Quinn, hand me the case, please," Cody said.

Quinn pulled it from his pocket and gave it to Cody. She lifted the unlocked lid and reread it to the group.

"**WILL** you find **THE** money?
No, it's not **INSIDE**.
LIES are in the **ASH**es.
Not a place to hide."

No one said anything for a few moments. Then Luke spoke up. "I still don't get it."

Quinn reread both messages to the others. "The riddles are similar," he said, once he was done. "See how some of the same words are used. But the lines of the poem are different."

153

Cody nodded, excited. "The same words in both messages are darker—and written in capital letters. There's got to be a reason."

"Okay, sooooo...," Luke said, thinking aloud. "It says, 'The money's not inside' and 'The lies are in the ashes.' It still doesn't tell us anything."

"Maybe not in the actual riddle," Cody said. "But maybe the highlighted words are the key." She handed her codebook to M.E. "Write this down."

M.E. flipped to a blank page. "Go."

"Okay, let's see. Write down *will*, *the*, *inside*, *ashes*, and *lies*. Those are the exact same words—the highlighted words—used in both notes."

M.E. printed the five words neatly on the paper, then read them aloud. "Will...the...inside...ashes ...lies."

Luke made a face, clearly puzzled. He took the metal case from Cody. "Wait a minute. This reminds me of my *grand-mère*'s puzzles. She loves anagrams—those mixed-up letters that make a word when they're unscrambled. She makes ana-grams out of my spelling words to help me learn them. Like this." He wrote the letters *Z. U. L. Z. E. P.* on Cody's notebook paper.

"Zulzep?" M.E. asked, reading the letters together.

"Unscramble the letters," Luke said, and handed her the pen.

Once he explained it, M.E. took only seconds to rearrange the letters. "Puzzle!"

"Yezzil!" Luke high-fived her. "So maybe the *words* are anagrams—all scrambled up—instead of the letters. Let me try rearranging them."

Luke took the notebook and pen from M.E. and went to work. He wrote out his first attempt.

"Will the ashes lie inside." He shook his head and drew a line through the sentence.

"Inside will lie the ashes." He scratched out another line.

"Ashes lie inside…"

Quinn held a hand up. "Wait, Luke. It's not *ashes*. Only the word *ash* is highlighted. Try again with just *ash*."

"Inside the ash lies will," Luke wrote, then he shrugged. "It still doesn't make sense."

"Maybe it's a question," Cody said. "Try starting with 'will.'"

"Will the ash lies inside… Will inside lies… Will lies inside the… ash?" Luke tried some other combinations, ending with the nonsensical phrase, *"Ash the inside lies will."*

"I think I got it!" Quinn said. He'd been standing opposite Luke and reading the message upside down and backward. "How about 'Will lies inside the ash'?"

"The will…," Cody slowly repeated, "lies… inside the ash… I think you're right, Quinn. It's *will*—a noun, not a verb, like in Skeleton Man's will. 'It lies'—it's hidden—'inside the… ash'?" The excitement in her voice faded. "But if the will lies

156

inside the ashes—"

"Then it's burned to a crisp," M.E. said, finishing her sentence.

Quinn frowned. "It doesn't say 'ashes,' remember? It says 'ash.'"

"Why not ashes?" Cody insisted. "You can't have just one ash." She looked out the broken window, trying to think what Skeleton Man could have meant. As her eyes moved from sculpture to sculpture, she went over the possibilities in her head. Where could Skeleton Man have hidden the will, if not in the ashes? In the ash can? In the ash tree...

Her eyes locked on the only tree sculpture in the yard that didn't look like the others. In addition to the cat sculptures, there were at least a dozen metal trees in the yard. They all looked pretty much the same—except one.

She pointed out the window. "See that tree out there?"

The others followed her finger.

"Notice how it's different from the others?" she continued.

Quinn shrugged. "Maybe Skeleton Man got tired of making the same old tree over and over. That one sort of looks like the one in your yard, Cody, only made out of metal."

Cody's eyes brightened. "Exactly! And guess what kind of tree that is."

Quinn frowned. "An ash tree?"

Luke's eyebrows lifted. "Dude! You think Skeleton Man's will is hidden in that tree sculpture?"

"I think we better find out before that crazy lady and her sidekick show up," Quinn suggested. "They said they'd be back. I'm guessing we don't have much time."

They raced outside to the sculpted ash tree. While the other trees had thin trunks and wide leaves, this metallic work of art had a broad trunk, spindly branches, and dangling leaves that tinkled in the breeze. Cody marveled at the effort that had gone into creating it. Skeleton Man, er, Mr. Skelton, might have been a strange hermit, but he was also quite the artist.

Quinn knelt down and checked the base of the tree. The others examined the branches and leaves, searching for some kind of secret opening, hidden compartment, or engraved message.

"I found something!" Quinn said. "Look, this part is loose, and it slides. There's a hole underneath." Quinn slid the metal plate at the base of the trunk aside and reached into the opening. Seconds later he withdrew a large envelope. On the front were the handwritten words, **_Last Will and Testament of Jake Skelton_**. Quinn held it up to show the others.

"OMG, you found it! Skeleton Man's will," M.E. said. "Open it. Hurry!"

"Do you think we should?" Cody asked. "Maybe we should take it to my dad, since he's a lawyer."

"Good idea," Luke said.

But Quinn didn't appear to be listening. He'd already lifted the back flap of the envelope and was pulling out a handful of folded papers.

"Quinn!" Cody said, shaking her head.

"I'm just taking a quick peek. Then we'll take it to your dad." Quinn unfolded the papers and scanned the top sheet for a few seconds before he spoke.

"Whoa," he said, refolding the papers and stuffing them back into the envelope. "You'll never guess how much money he has. And who he's giving it to!"

"Shhh!" Cody said. She glanced around. "Those strangers might hear you. Let's get out of here." The kids checked one last time for spies, then ran from the yard.

None of them noticed the beat-up old car parked across the street, nor the two passengers scrunched down in the front seats.

Chapter 15

Cody and her friends headed for the clubhouse to hide the will until they could get Cody's father to look it over. She knew her dad was in court all day. On the way, Quinn told them the details of the will: that the old man had planned to donate his money—over a hundred thousand dollars—to the SPCA. Cody was stunned at the amount and glad it would be going to a good cause—to help animals.

Just as they arrived, Cody noticed something odd about the door to the clubhouse. She put a finger to her lips and pointed to the bottom of the door.

Luke held up a hand. "I'll check it out," he whispered, and knelt down to examine the marks. He stood up. "Looks like someone's been kicking at the door."

Luke glanced around the area. Cody figured whoever it was—probably Matt the Brat—was long gone. He'd been obsessed with their clubhouse ever since he'd followed them to the secluded area one day. Cody knew it was only a matter of time before he brought the right tool and broke in. Matt the Brat was the main reason they hid their important stuff under the metal floor.

"Doesn't look like whoever it was got inside," Luke said. "The chain and lock are still here." He spun the combination lock, opened it, and yanked open the clubhouse door. After Luke checked the inside, the others followed him in.

Quinn lifted part of the aluminum floor. "We've got to hide this will until your dad can look at it, Cody." He placed the will in the hole and recovered the floor. "Meanwhile, we've got to—"

Cody shushed Quinn. She thought she'd heard a noise outside.

The kids froze, their eyes glued to the clubhouse door.

A loud thud hit the door, startling them. M.E. screamed, then covered her mouth.

The sound was followed by another loud thud, then another.

Someone was trying to break the door down!

Before the Code Busters could do anything, the door came crashing in, splintering into pieces that narrowly missed Cody and M.E. They all ducked and covered their heads. When the dust settled, they looked up to see what appeared to be a giant flower garden standing at the entryway.

Peeking around from behind was a short, balding man.

Jezebel and Jasper!

The kids scooted back against the clubhouse wall in terror. By the looks on the intruders' faces, this was not a friendly visit. How had they found them? Cody wondered. She tried to duck past Jezebel, but the Flower Lady caught her by her shirt and yanked her back. In that split second, she'd had time to catch a glimpse of freedom. Jezebel pushed Cody against the far wall. The woman was not only large; she was strong. Cody rubbed her head where it had hit the side of the billboard wall. She felt dampness on her fingers and held up her hand.

Blood!

"Where is it?" Jezebel growled at them. "We know you have it."

"Yeah," Jasper added. "We were watching you from across the street."

"Where's what?" Luke asked, pretending ignorance. Cody knew he was stalling for time.

"You know what I'm talking about," Jezebel shouted. "The will! Give it here!"

Quinn shook his head. "We…We don't know what you're talking about. We don't have a will."

Jezebel looked at Jasper, who'd remained standing quietly behind her. He stepped forward and grabbed Quinn's arm, holding it behind Quinn's back. "You better tell us, kid," Jasper squeaked, "or Jezebel here will sit on you. And you don't want that." Jasper grinned, until he caught a sharp look from Jezebel, who apparently didn't like the reference to her size.

Meanwhile, Cody tried to think. The bump on her head Jezebel had given her had made her mad, and she was determined to outwit these money-hungry creeps.

"Okay, okay, I'll tell you!" she said. The others shot her a look. She rubbed the bottom of her chin sideways, and the kids relaxed a little. She'd just given them the American Sign Language sign for "lie."

"That a girl," Jezebel said. Jasper let go of Quinn's arm.

"We...hid it," Cody continued. "In a cave...in the forest." She pointed up the hill where the Code Busters had gone exploring one day and found an abandoned cave.

Jezebel frowned at her suspiciously. "Where exactly?"

"I'll draw you a map," Cody said. She got out a sheet of paper and drew a map, labeling landmarks along the way—"**G**o **O**ut. **T**urn uphill. go **A**round **P**it. Look for **A N**atural cave."

Code Buster's Solution found on p. 207.

She showed it to Jezebel. "Just follow this map. The will is hidden inside the cave."

Jezebel snatched the map out of Cody's hands, glanced at it, and threw it on the ground. It landed facedown.

166

"Forget the map. You're going to show me. Let's go," Jezebel demanded.

Perfect, Cody thought, as she knelt down and flipped over the paper so the others could see the coded map. She's following my plan. Cody stood up, leaving the map lying on the floor in plain view.

"I said, let's go," Jezebel repeated. "You're going to show us."

Cody glanced at the others, then nodded to the map that lay on the floor. Quinn looked at it, then smiled.

He'd figured out her message by reading the capitalized letters.

"Jasper," Jezebel continued. "Stay here and watch these brats. If I don't come back with that will...well, you know what to do." She sneered at Cody.

Jasper nodded.

"Now tie them up," Jezebel added.

Jasper pulled a long rope out of the backpack he'd been carrying and began to tie up the other three. He turned them back-to-back-to-back and looped the rope around their torsos, then tied their hands. Cody watched in horror as her three friends were made helpless in front of her eyes. M.E. had begun to cry but was trying hard to blink back the tears. Cody saw Luke whisper something to comfort her.

"Don't worry, guys," Cody said to her friends. "I'll show her where the will is and be right back. Then they'll leave us alone." She turned to Jezebel. "Won't you?"

Jezebel ignored her. Instead, she tied a piece of rope to Cody's thin wrist and tied the other end to her own. Then she gave Cody a shove out the door and followed her.

Moving slowly, Cody headed up the hill toward the cave, wondering if the mountain lion made it his home. She hoped the walk would give her time to think of a way to get out of this mess. Otherwise, she'd either end up in the hospital like Skeleton Man, or worse—as a snack for a mountain lion.

By the time they neared the cave, Jezebel was wheezing and puffing hard. She'd had to rest every few steps along the way. Cody was barely winded, but she held her breath when she thought she heard a noise coming from inside the cave. She couldn't be sure, since Jezebel was grunting and panting so loudly.

"Why do you want the will so bad?" Cody asked, stalling for time. "He didn't leave his money to you guys."

"Duh," Jezebel wheezed. "That's why we have to find it before anyone else does—so we can destroy it and replace it with another will that's more beneficial to us."

"You made a fake will?" Cody asked.

Jezebel smirked. "Yeah, it's all part of our plan.

Once Jake is out of the way, we'll tie up that last loose end."

"What do you mean, out of the way?"

"He's old, you know. It's time for him to go. We're just trying to help him get there a little faster."

It was obvious to Cody now: Jezebel and Jasper had set the fire at Skeleton Man's house.

"Enough with the questions," Jezebel said, still trying to catch her breath. "Now go get the will."

"It's in there." Cody pointed toward the cave opening with her free hand.

"So, go on. Get it. Now!" Jezebel huffed.

Cody had an idea and yanked on the rope that connected her to Jezebel. "It's...way in there. You'll have to untie me or come with me—if you're not afraid of mountain lions."

"Mountain lions?" Jezebel gulped and glanced around nervously. "There's no way I'm going in there if there's mountain lions around here." She untied the rope around her wrist, freeing Cody. "Now get on in there and get that will, unless you want something to happen to your pals."

Cody knew if she ran off, Jezebel and Jasper would do something terrible to her friends. She had no choice but to go inside and possibly face a hungry mountain lion.

Cody picked up a nearby stone and threw it into the cave.

"What are you doing?" Jezebel yelled. "I said, get in there."

"Just…checking to make sure the mountain lion isn't in there," Cody said.

Jezebel's eyes narrowed. Cody took a step inside. Then another. Then another, until she was just out of site of Jezebel. Once inside, she made a low guttural noise, then screamed, "Mountain lion!" and ran out of the cave opening.

Before Jezebel could even move, Cody was halfway down the hill at a full run. The last thing she heard was the shrill cry of a very frightened woman, running as fast as her legs would carry her, no doubt certain a mountain lion was about to attack her.

By the time Cody reached the clubhouse, she had another plan. Still screaming "Mountain lion!" she ran into the clubhouse and frantically repeated them, "Mountain lion! Mountain lion!"

Jasper stared at Cody. "What are you talking about? Where's Jezebel?"

"Mountain lion!" she puffed. "It's...It's after Jezebel. Didn't you hear about it? It was all over the news."

Quinn, Luke, and M.E., still tied together back-to-back-to-back, began yelling, "We've got to get outta here!"

Jasper took one look at their terrified faces and bolted out the door. Cody watched him half run, half fall down the hill. He was actually running *away* from the "mountain lion" and his beloved Jezebel.

Cody dashed over to her friends and untied the ropes as quickly as she could.

"Did you really see a mountain lion?" M.E. asked, with a look of terror still on her face.

Cody shook her head. "No, thank goodness. But as long as Jezebel and Jasper *think* there is one, it should give us time to get out of here."

Moments later the kids were headed down the hill toward the relative safety of civilization. There was no sign of Jasper—or Jezebel—along the way.

"Shoot!" Quinn said when they reached the street. "I forgot the will! It's still hidden under the floor. Anyone can go in there now that the door has been knocked down."

"We'll go back for it later," Luke said. "When we've got some backup."

"You're right about that," Cody added. She

glanced back at the forest, glad she remembered about the mountain lion—and happy she hadn't really seen one.

She didn't like the idea of anyone—even Jezebel—being eaten by a mountain lion.

Chapter 16

Half an hour later Cody and the Code Busters gang headed for the clubhouse, backed up by two Berkeley police officers: Sergeant Carl Price and Lieutenant Susan Jones—Cody's mom. Tana had wanted to come along, but Cody's mom had said it was too dangerous with a couple of ruthless thieves, not to mention a possible mountain lion, on the loose. She had asked their father, who'd gotten out of court early, to watch Cody's sister.

So far there had been no sign of Jasper and Jezebel. But as the group neared the clubhouse, Cody's worst fear was realized. Someone—Jezebel and Jasper?—had smashed down the remaining walls, destroying the clubhouse.

"Oh, no!" Cody said, shocked to see their secret place turned into a pile of trash.

Quinn shook his head, while Luke just stared at the remains. M.E. looked near tears.

"Do you know who did this?" Sergeant Price asked, surveying the damage.

"Probably Jasper and Jezebel, or maybe Matt," Cody said, blinking back her own tears.

"Who are Jasper and Jezebel?" Cody's mom asked.

"I told you," Cody said. "They're supposedly Skeleton Man's—I mean, Mr. Skelton's—relatives. They've been trying to find his will. They plan to replace it with a fake one so they can inherit Mr.

Skelton's fortune—" Cody stopped and blinked several times before continuing to explain all that had happened.

Cody's mom put an arm around her daughter. "You guys were smart to run away. We'll send some officers to look for the two of them." She turned to Quinn. "What's this about a will, Quinn?"

Quinn glanced at Cody, as if to make sure it was all right to tell Lieutenant Jones. Cody nodded. "Well, we found Skeleton Man's will—I mean, Mr. Skelton's will—hidden in his yard."

"What were you doing in his yard?" Cody's mom asked, turning her attention to her daughter.

"He sent us a message," Cody said. "From his bedroom window. It said 'help' in semaphore code, only we didn't figure it out until later. We decoded another one of his messages, and that's what led us to the will."

"Yeah. He left clues. It was like he knew about our

Code Busters Club," M.E. added, wiping her eyes.

Sergeant Price glanced at the pile of rubble, then turned to the kids. "You guys could have been killed, you know. You're lucky you got away when you did. Now...where's this so-called will?"

Quinn glanced at the others. He was about to give away a top secret—the clubhouse hiding place. But Cody knew he had no choice. Together the kids pushed away the broken walls of the clubhouse until the metal floor was visible. Quinn and Luke knelt down and together lifted up part of the floor.

Quinn reached inside the hole in the dirt and pulled out the envelope. He removed the papers he'd hidden inside just before Jezebel and Jasper had arrived.

"Here," he said, handing the contents to Sergeant Price. "Mr. Skelton is planning to leave all his money to the SPCA—to take care of his cats. I guess his relatives don't like animals that much. They wanted the money for themselves."

"What money?" Cody's mom asked. "I thought the man was practically destitute."

"Not really." Cody smiled at her mom. "The will says he has more than a hundred thousand dollars."

The cops looked at each other with raised eyebrows.

"Dudes...I mean, officers," Luke said. "Those relatives of his were the ones who burned down Skeleton Man's house. They tried to kill him."

Cody's breath caught in her throat. She suddenly remembered something Jezebel had said on the way to the cave:

"It's time for him to go. We're just trying to help him get there a little faster."

Maybe they aren't finished yet, Cody thought. "Come on!"

"What is it, Cody?" her mom asked.

"We've got to get to the hospital," Cody insisted. "Mr. Skelton may be in trouble!"

"What kind of trouble?" Cody's mom asked.

"Jezebel and Jasper said they were going to help Mr. Skelton...die."

With lights and sirens blaring, the squad car containing two officers and four kids sped to Berkeley General Hospital, where Jake Skelton had been taken. When they arrived, ten minutes later, they rushed from the car and through the automatic front doors, to the front desk. Sergeant Price asked a volunteer for Skelton's room and was given a number. As he headed down the hall, the Code Busters started after him.

"Wait! You kids can't go in there," said a nearby nurse, waving a clipboard at them. "No kids allowed until visiting hours."

Cody's mom turned to the woman, her hand pointing to her badge. Cody thought her mom looked cool and was proud of her.

"They're with us," she said, speaking with

authority. The nurse glanced at Lieutenant Jones's badge and nodded reluctantly. The kids stifled grins as they caught up with Sergeant Price.

The sergeant opened the door to Jake Skelton's room and stuck his head inside. Cody couldn't see with Sergeant Price blocking the door.

Then she heard, "Hold it right there!"

Sergeant Price pushed the door wide open and marched in.

Cody and her friends rushed inside, but Cody froze as she took in the situation. Hovering over a frail old man were Jasper and Jezebel. Jezebel's arms and legs were covered with scratches.

"What the heck is going on?" Jasper asked, standing up straight and pulling his hands away from Jake Skelton. He held a sheet of paper in one hand and a pen in the other. "This is a private room. You have no business—"

Cody's mom flashed her badge at them. Jasper shut his mouth.

Cody took the paper from Jasper's hand and read it aloud: "'Last Will and Testament of Jake Skelton.' This is it! The fake will. I think they are trying to force him to sign it!"

She looked at the old man lying in the bed. His eyes were closed. He wasn't moving. Cody's mom rang the emergency buzzer.

"Did they kill him?" M.E. squealed, then covered her mouth with her hands.

"You two, you're under arrest," Sergeant Price said to the couple.

"On what grounds?" Jezebel bellowed.

"We'll start with suspicion of attempted murder," Sergeant Price answered.

Jasper and Jezebel slowly raised their arms. Cody's mom seized the bottle of pills Jezebel had been hiding in her tight fist.

"You have the right to remain silent," Sergeant Price began, as he pulled out his handcuffs and cuffed Jezebel to Jasper. Jezebel winced in pain.

"You have the right—"

"We ain't done nothing!" Jezebel screeched. "We were just visiting our dear sick cousin."

Lieutenant Jones read the label on the medicine bottle. "These don't look like vitamins," she said. "Like the sergeant said, it looks more like attempted murder, not to mention arson, fraud, extortion, forgery ..." She continued the list as Sergeant Price shoved the handcuffed pair through the door and into the hall. Cody heard Jezebel moan with each step down the corridor.

The kids turned their attention to Cody's mom, who was holding Skeleton Man's frail, mottled wrist. She appeared to be feeling for a pulse.

Where is that nurse? Cody thought, her heart racing.

Then, to her amazement, she saw one of Skeleton Man's eyes flutter open.

Bloodshot, the eye glanced around the room.

Cody's mom held his hand. "Your so-called

cousins are gone, Mr. Skelton. In fact, they've been arrested. The fire department found evidence of arson at your home. They'll probably be charged with setting fire to your house. And it looks like we caught them trying to forge your name to a fraudulent will." She didn't mention the bottle of pills Jezebel had had hidden in her hand.

Jake Skelton's eye narrowed. Cody wondered if he understood what her mother had said.

Then one side of his mouth opened. It looked to Cody like he was trying to say something.

"Is he all right?" Cody whispered to her mother. "Can't he talk?"

"No, dear," Cody's mom said softly. "He had a stroke several months ago."

"What's a stroke?" M.E. asked.

Cody's mom took a deep breath. "A stroke is like a brain attack. It happens when an artery is blocked, usually by a blood clot or a broken blood vessel. Sometimes, when this happens, it affects brain cells. It can impair motor skills, usually on one side of the body. Mr. Skelton's left arm and leg aren't working properly, and his speech is affected."

"Is he going to …?" M.E. whispered. She seemed unable to say the word *die.*

"Not necessarily, dear. But he's been doing physical therapy to help improve his movement. The fire didn't help any."

"Will he be able to talk again?" Cody asked.

"Hopefully, with speech therapy."

Cody's mom turned to the man lying in bed. "How are you feeling, Mr. Skelton?"

To Cody's surprise, he lifted his right hand and gave a thumbs-up. The right side of his face lifted into a half grin.

"Mr. Skelton, these kids here found your will," Cody's mom said. "Your life—and your money— are safe, thanks to them."

Jake Skelton raised his thumb again.

"And so is your cat—Punkin. I mean, Francis Scott," Cody added. "I'm going to take care of him until you get well." She looked at her mom. Lieutenant Jones nodded. "The rest are at the SPCA, safe and sound."

Jake Skelton eyed Cody, then crooked his right index finger at her, signaling her to come closer.

Cody stepped forward nervously. She hadn't been around old people much. And never around a person who was half paralyzed.

Jake Skelton reached out his right hand, and she took it. His hand felt dry, cool, and bony, but there was warmth in his gentle squeeze. Cody smiled at him.

"I'm Cody. I live across the street from you." She turned to the other Code Busters and introduced them one by one. "This is Quinn—he's your next-door neighbor."

Quinn took off his sunglasses and gave a wave. Jake eyed him.

"This is Luke, and that's MariaElena. We call her M.E. We formed the Code Busters Club because we like to solve puzzles and decipher codes. That's how we finally figured out that you were in trouble, and where your will was hidden."

Jake Skelton gave another half smile. The rest of his face didn't move.

"I have a question." Quinn stepped closer and rubbed his hair nervously. "Did you used to work for the CIA? 'Cause that's what I want to do when I grow up."

The old man shook his head and frowned with one eyebrow. Then he lifted his good hand and began to gesture.

"He's trying to tell us something," Quinn said to the others.

They watched intently as Jake Skelton bent his hand into a claw shape and pretended to scratch the air. Cody paid close attention. Having used sign language with her deaf sister, she was getting good at reading facial expressions and body language.

"Do you have an itch?" M.E. asked, moving closer. Jake Skelton shook his head. Then he put his right hand up to his temple and flapped it.

"Ear?" Luke asked.

He shook his head again. Finally, he moved his hand next to his mouth, and opened and closed his hand.

"Talk?" Quinn guessed.

Jake Skelton closed his eyes. Cody knew they weren't getting it. She thought for a moment, then said, "Obviously, he's trying to tell us something. All we have to do is decode his gestures. First he made a scratching gesture. Like a cat. The second was like an ear, but instead of pointing to his ear, he held his hand up, like the ear was standing up. Kind of like a horse's ear. And the third thing sort of looked like a duck's bill, opening and closing."

One of Jake Skelton's eyes widened. A tear glistened.

"A cat. A horse. A duck. So what do they all have in common? They're all animals." Cody looked at Jake Skelton.

Skelton nodded and half smiled.

"Did you work with animals?" Quinn asked. "Like in the zoo or circus or something?"

Skelton shook his head. Then he raised his right arm, pointed his finger, and brought it over to his motionless left arm.

"It looks like he's giving himself a shot," Quinn said, looking at the others.

"Do you need some medicine?" Luke asked.

Jake Skelton shook his head.

"Do you need a doctor?" M.E. asked.

Jake Skelton shook his head again. Then he pointed to himself.

Cody lit up. "Were you a doctor?"

He nodded.

"An animal doctor? A vet?" she asked.

Jake Skelton raised a thumbs-up.

"Cool! No wonder you had so many cats," M.E. said.

At that moment, the nurse entered the room and gave them all a "time's up" look.

"We'd better be going, kids," Cody's mom said. "Dr. Skelton needs his rest."

The Code Busters nodded. Each one patted the old man on his right arm. Cody thought how much their view of Skeleton Man—Dr. Skelton— had changed in such a short time. Instead of being the scary hermit with too many cats and weird sculptures who kept to himself, he was actually a retired veterinarian who loved animals and did metal art. They just hadn't taken the time to get to know him. And after his stroke, he became more reclusive.

"I've got an idea," Cody said, then turned to Skeleton Man. "You're really good at making gestures, Dr. Skelton. I'm teaching my friends sign language. How about we come and show you some signs so you can communicate until your speech comes back?"

Jake Skelton gave a half grin. He started to say something, then tears filled his eyes again.

Cody moved closer. "Here. I'll teach you your first sign." She thought about teaching him the sign for "friend," but that would take two hands. "I know…do this." She pulled some imaginary whiskers from the side of her face. "That's 'cat,' in American Sign Language. After all, a cat was the key to this whole puzzle."

Jake Skelton repeated the sign with his bony fingers.

"Tomorrow we'll teach you the alphabet. Then you'll be able to say anything you want. And then maybe you can tell us how you knew we could help you when you wrote those semaphores on your window."

Chapter 17

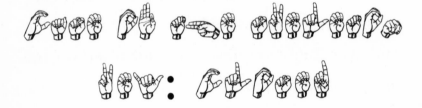

"That was really nice of you kids, offering to teach Dr. Skelton sign language," Cody's mom said later that night over spaghetti dinner. She'd invited the rest of the Code Busters to join them.

"Uttle bah fuffle," Quinn said. Cody figured that was mouth-full-of-garlic-bread code for "It'll be fun."

"Yeah," she said, "and I get to take care of Punkin until Dr. Skelton gets out of the hospital. I just wish I could keep him."

"Well, guys," Cody's mom said. "I got a call from Dr. Skelton's caregiver while you guys were hauling your stuff down from the old clubhouse."

The four looked at one another. Cody's fork hung in midair. She felt a sinking feeling in her stomach.

"Is he okay?" Cody asked.

"Oh yes, he's doing well. But he had a message for you all. He typed it on a laptop the caregiver brought him. She read his message to me over the phone."

"What did it say?" Luke asked.

"He said he's going to use some of his money to help you build a new clubhouse. Once he learned about everything you guys did to help him, he wanted to do something to thank you."

"Whoa!" Quinn said. "That's *awesome*. A brand-new clubhouse."

M.E. clapped. "That's totally cool!"

Cody looked at Luke. To her surprise, Luke frowned.

"What's wrong, Luke?" Cody asked. "You want a new clubhouse, don't you?"

"Sure, of course. But there's something I still don't get. We thought he worked for the CIA, but he turned out to be a vet. So what about all those puzzles? And that certificate on the wall? 'Sup with that?"

"Oh, I finally figured that out," Quinn said. "The letters on that certificate were supposed to say *SPCA*, not *CIA*. He got them for rescuing cats. The one we found was burned, except for a couple of letters—*CA*. We just read it wrong."

"But what about the *I*? I know I saw *CIA*," Luke insisted.

"It was a smudge—soot from the fire. I thought the *I* was a little odd at the time because it didn't look exactly like the other letters."

"Dude, nothing in this case was what it seemed," Luke said, shaking his head.

"So why did he create all those puzzles?" M.E. asked.

"I know the answer to that," Cody's mom spoke up. "He explained it to the caregiver who read his note to me. He knew his distant cousins, Jasper and Jezebel, would come after his money someday. They were always asking him about it. So he hid the will and left coded messages leading to its location. He figured Jasper and Jezebel were not smart enough to figure out the puzzles. And he knew you guys were into puzzles and codes. He heard you talking in Quinn's yard and found out about your club. Remember you said he was often watching you?"

"He's pretty amazing." Cody took her plate to the kitchen. The other three did the same.

"Did you hear anything about Matt the Brat?" Quinn asked Cody's mom.

"The sergeant and I went over there and talked to him and his parents. He said he had nothing to do with destroying the clubhouse, except that he threw a rock at it."

"Why would he do that?" Cody asked.

"Maybe he was jealous of you guys. Maybe he really wants to belong to your club and just doesn't know how to ask."

Cody thought about her mom's words. She was probably right, but Cody still didn't want him in the club. Maybe they could include him in another way. She'd have to think about it. He could be so annoying!

"Listen, you guys, go do your homework," Cody's mom said. "I'll do these dishes. How about some brownies later?"

Cody remembered the brownies that went flying around the cafeteria earlier and grimaced. "Thanks, Mom, but could we have ice cream instead?"

Cody led her friends upstairs to her bedroom. She

sat at her desk while Luke and Quinn flopped on the bed and M.E. wiggled into a beanbag chair. She turned on her computer to check her IMs, texts, and e-mail messages before starting her math homework. It had been hours since she'd last checked, and she was expecting a note from her dad about Jake Skelton's will.

She signed on, clicked "Mail," and watched as a dozen messages loaded into her file. The first few were spam, which she quickly deleted. The next two were answers to some homework questions she'd requested from the "Homework Help" site. Three more came from newsgroups she belonged to—SignChat, PuzzlePlace, and MysteryMansion. The last message was from her dad.

To: CodeRed@CodeBustersClub.com

From: MatthewJones@JonesLaw.com

Subj: Skelton's Will

Message: Hi Dakota. It's ur dad here. Y R U on

the computer instead of doing ur homework???
JK!! ;)

Cody smiled at her dad's attempt to use messaging code before she read on.

Skelton's will is authentic. I'll keep it here in a safe at my office until I see him tomorrow. Nice work, helping him out like that. You and the Code Busters, right?
TTUL8R. Love, Dad

Cody gave a sigh of relief at the news. Case closed. She pulled up the last message and caught her breath. The little hairs on the back of her neck prickled as she scanned the cryptic message.

To: CodeRed@CodeBustersClub.com
From: TheShadow@Question.com
Subject: Treasure Hunt

Message:

In darkness yon,

A shrouded night covers island mists.

Those hallowed, sunken, tired souls,

Lively ghosts hope you'll see...

Alone a local treasure.

—Z

Cody stared at her computer screen. Was this supposed to be some kind of poem from someone who called himself TheShadow? If it was, it made no sense. "Hey, guys. Did one of you send this to me?" The others looked at the screen and shook their heads.

"It looks like an old-fashioned poem. What does it mean?" M.E. asked.

"I'm not sure. It's from someone called the Shadow."

"Maybe it's a code," Quinn said. "See? Some of the letters are in bold."

Cody highlighted the message and copied it to a new document. Then she removed all the letters that weren't in bold, leaving:

I dare y ou t ov is it

The ha un ted

Li ght ho u se

on a lca tra

Z

"Try sounding it out," Luke said, then began with "I dare..."

Moments later he had translated the coded poem.

Code Buster's Solution found on p. 207.

"Sounds cool," Cody said. "When can we go?"

CODE BUSTER'S

Key Book
&
Solutions

Finger Spelling:

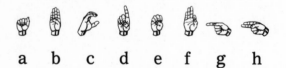

a   b   c   d   e   f   g   h

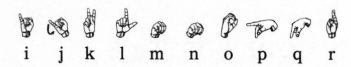

i   j   k   l   m   n   o   p   q   r

s   t   u   v   w   x   y   z

Morse Code:

A .-	**H**	**O** ---	**V** ...-
B -...	**I** ..	**P** .--.	**W** .--
C -.-.	**J** .---	**Q** --.-	**X** -..-
D -..	**K** -.-	**R** .-.	**Y** -.--
E .	**L** .-..	**S** ...	**Z** --..
F ..-.	**M** --	**T** -	
G --.	**N** -.	**U** ..-	

Caesar's Cipher:

1	2	3	4	5	6	7	8	9
c	o	d	e	b	u	s	t	r

10	11	12	13	14	15	16	17
z	i	n	l	k	m	a	y

18	19	20	21	22	23	24	25	26
x	h	j	f	g	p	v	w	q

Semaphores:

a b c d e f g h i

j k l m n o p q r

s t u v w x y z

Braille Alphabet:

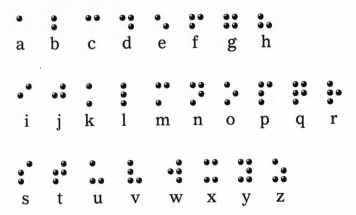

a b c d e f g h

i j k l m n o p q r

s t u v w x y z

Chapter 1

Alphanumeric code: 10-15-9-14   20-8-5

3-15-4-5   2-21-19-20-5-18-19   3-12-21-2

Join the Code Buster's Club.

Chapter 2

Finger spelling:

Fire. Across the street.

Need to dress. Dad coming.

Chapter 3

ABC code: **Meet me at the clubhouse after school. Lock and key.**

Chapter 4

Caesar's cipher:

3-2-12-8 21-2-9-22-4-8 8-2 15-4-4-8 15-4 16-8

8-19-4 21-13-16-22-23-2-13-4 16-21-8-4-9

7-1-19-2-2-13 15.4.

Don't forget to meet me at the flagpole after school. M.E.

Chapter 5

Morse code: **-.. .---**

D. J.

Chapter 6

Text message translation: **What's up, Red? Good luck on your spelling test. You go, girl! Talk to you later. Pop. Hugs**

    Hi Pop. Thanks. See you later. Hugs, Red

Consonant code: **Meet at the library at 1900 hours.**

Chapter 7

$25 + 36 = 61 + 81 = 142 + 400 = 542 - 37 =$ **505**

Chapter 8

Double Dutch: Syllables are broken up, and "ag" is added in between. For example, "Not" would be "Nag-ot," tonight would be "to-nag-ite."

Not tonight. Tomorrow.

Chapter 10

Finger spelling:

Thieves

Chapter 11

Morse code: **SOS. Matt in caf. Need help. SOS.**

Chapter 13

Semaphores: **Under couch**
Braille: **Floor space**

Chapter 15

"Go Out. Turn uphill. go Around Pit.
Look for A Natural cave." **Got a plan.**

Chapter 17

**I dare you to visit the haunted lighthouse
on Alcatraz...**

<u>Finger spelling:</u>

<u>Chapter Title Translations</u>

Chapter 1 *The Clawed Hand*

Chapter 2 *Up in Flames*

Chapter 3 *The Secret Message*

Chapter 4 *The Coded Note*

Chapter 5 *The Stealthy Stalker*

Chapter 6 *A Secret Meeting*

Chapter 7 *Shadow in the Stacks*

Chapter 8 *A Secret Place*

Chapter 9 *Out of the Ashes*

Chapter 10 *The Black Ghost*

Chapter 11 *Cafeteria Caper*

Chapter 12 *Food Fight*

Chapter 13 *What Lies Beneath*

Chapter 14 *The Curious Cat*

Chapter 15 *Mountain Lion!*

Chapter 16 *The Skeleton Key*

Chapter 17 *Case of the Skeleton Key: Closed*

For more adventures with the Code Busters Club, go to www.CodeBustersClub.com.

There you'll find:

1. Full dossiers for Cody, Quinn, Luke, and M.E.
2. Their blogs
3. More codes
4. More coded messages to solve
5. Clues to the next book
6. A map of the Code Busters neighborhood, school, and mystery
7. A contest to win your name in the next Code Busters book.

SUGGESTIONS FOR TEACHERS

Kids love codes. They will want to "solve" the codes in this novel before looking up the solutions. This means they will be practicing skills that are necessary to their class work in several courses, but in a non-pressured way.

The codes in this book vary in level of difficulty so there is something for students of every ability. The codes move from a simple code wheel—Caesar's Cipher wheel—to more widely accepted "code" languages such as Morse code, semaphore and Braille.

In a mathematics classroom, the codes in this book can easily be used as motivational devices to teach problem-solving and reasoning skills. Both of these have become important elements in the curriculum at all grade levels. The emphasis throughout the book on regarding codes as *patterns* gives students a great deal of practice in one of the primary strategies of problem solving. The strategy of "Looking for a Pattern" is basic to much of mathematics. The resolving of codes demonstrates how important patterns are. These codes can lead to discussions of the logic behind why they "work," (problem solving). The teacher can then have the students create their own codes (problem formulation) and try sending secret messages to one another, while other students try to "break the code." Developing and resolving these new codes will require a great deal of careful reasoning on the part of the students. The class might also wish to do some practical research in statistics, to determine which letters occur most frequently in the English language. (*E*, *T*, *A*, *O*, and *N* are the first five most widely used letters and should appear most often in coded messages.)

This book may also be used in other classroom areas of study such as social studies, with its references to code-breaking machines, American Sign Language, and Braille. This book raises questions such as, "Why would semaphore be important today? Where is it still used?"

In the English classroom, spelling is approached as a "deciphering code." The teacher may also suggest the students do some outside reading. They might read a biography of Samuel Morse or Louis Braille, or even the Sherlock Holmes mystery "The Adventure of the Dancing Men."

This book also refers to modern texting on cell phones and computers as a form of code. Students could explain what the various "code" abbreviations they use mean today and why they are used.   —*Dr. Stephen Krulik*

Dr. Stephen Krulik has a distinguished career as a professor of mathematics education. Professor emeritus at Temple University, he received the 2011 Lifetime Achievement Award from the National Council of Teachers of Mathematics.

ACKNOWLEDGMENTS

Thanks to my outstanding critique group: Colleen Casey, Janet Finsilver, Staci McLaughlin, Ann Parker, and Carole Price. I couldn't have done it without the help and support of my husband Tom, my mother Connie Pike, and my family, Mike and Rebecca Melvin, and Matt and Sue Warner. Finally, a special thanks to my wonderful agent, Stefanie Von Borstel, and my incredible editors, Regina Griffin, Erin Molta, and everyone at Egmont USA.